RIVERSIDE DAYDREAMS

RIVERSIDE DAYDREAMS

A COLLECTION OF SHORT FICTION

BY TYLER J RIGG

proving
press

Book Design & Production:
Columbus Publishing Lab
www.ColumbusPublishingLab.com

Copyright © 2021 by
Tyler J. Rigg
LCCN: 2021921068

Cover design by Abigail Tabler

Paperback ISBN: 978-1-63337-561-1
E-Book ISBN: 978-1-63337-562-8

Printed in the United States of America
1 3 5 7 9 10 8 6 4 2

For my wonderful and supportive parents.

Contents

Heartland

IN MY SPRINGTIME DREAMS, I would often see a café laid out across a railroad bridge. Patrons sat in two long rows of tables, with passerby and baristas between them. Not far below were rushing, crystalline waters. I heard people laughing and the soft buzz of conversations. Sunlight gleamed down on the café, fractured by the trestle's iron beams. Westward, the railroad carried on, aiming true toward a bright and beautiful countryside.

Short North

I USED TO KNOW A GUY FROM COLLEGE, unpopular and quiet, who lived on the second floor of a shop on a crowded corridor. Bar lights across the street burst through his window every hour of every night, flashing red, green, yellow, blue—painful and loud. The thunder of music and arrhythmic, grating yells were just below his window. He could never hear exactly what people were yelling about. They went on and on and on until the early hours of the morning. For months, he would wake up in an angry sweat, his head throbbing while he imagined the flashing spectrum everywhere he looked—a colorful, roaring tornado.

One night, he wandered into the galaxy of lights and stood in the middle. It was louder and brighter than he could've imagined from behind his window. Shaking with anxiety, he forced his mouth to open. He said hello to the bartenders and the servers and everyone who met his gaze. Then people talked to the guy. Strangers shared stories with him and laughed along with his jokes. He forgot about the tornado. And he smiled most of the night until he was back home. He lay in his bed, and the lights and the noises were no more than a lullaby floating him into a pacific sleep.

Night Sweats

A YOUNG WOMAN WOKE to the rumble of nearing thunder. There were flashes through her window and billowing, violet clouds that echoed the fever running through her veins. She stood up, feeling torrid and lost, and left for the front door while her husband slept with an empty bottle on the couch. His snores were drowned by the drumming of rain. She watched him for only a second, having already cried because of him the evening before. Then she left her umbrella by the doorway and began walking under the arched glow of streetlights.

Along a bright and quiet street, a homeless man sat outside a diner, his shoulders hunched as rain drizzled off the overhang. He smiled at the woman as she passed. She smiled back and offered him a five-dollar bill. "Bless your heart," he said. "I gotta ask, though…why you walking by yourself? And when it's stormin' like this?"

She breathed in deep the fresh, saturated air. "I don't mind," she said. "On nights like these, I just want to feel the rain."

November Wind

TWO OLD MEN PLAY CHESS next to me in a coffee shop. One tells me that a November wind is coming. "It has the last four years," he says. "It was real windy yesterday, you know. Snowed, too." A rush of icy air fills the room as the front door opens and closes. The man shivers and sips his steaming latte. "Every year," he murmurs. He asks me what I'm reading. I show him the book cover: *A Moveable Feast*. "Oh, I had to read that in high school," he says. "That's some timeless work, right there. Enjoy it." I tell him I will.

The sun sets on the shop, spilling amber through the back windows. I order another coffee and decide to stay, despite the coming cold and dark evening.

Floored

I WAS BLIND DRUNK; reeled, crashing onto the hardwood and sick the entire night. I couldn't get up from the floor, but you lay next to me, tender hand on my chest as I breathed slow and let your warmth soothe me. "What am I doing?" I said. "I'm sorry." I really, truly felt sorry. You told me that you couldn't leave me alone. And God, what I put you through. I don't know why you were there. I don't know why you stayed. But I loved the chaos and every moment full of sickening richness. I loved you again like I had before, but I couldn't say it and I didn't. I wish I had.

The sun came in the cold morning, and I lay back in your car to watch the clouds drift by while you took me home in silence. I couldn't stop apologizing. You were strong and told me to stop. You cared for me, but you couldn't have cared less about us.

Later, I slept, consumed by dreams of bittersweet half-love and the pain of living within a memory.

The Weathergirl

AT 6 P.M., BUSTER NEARY FELT A RUMBLE in his stomach. He had the same amount of cake and ice cream as everyone else at the birthday party, but he was 71 and the oldest person there. He was eating only a fraction of the sugar he had as a younger man. So, Buster's family sat in the living room together and talked and laughed while he watched from the dining room table. With one hand around a cup of water, he leaned back in his chair. His granddaughter Emma had just finished opening her gifts. She was flipping through each page of a book she'd received. It was full of photos, but she spent minutes at a time focused on each page. The adults continued talking to each other all around her. Buster took a deep breath. His head was swimming. He stood up slowly and stepped out onto the porch. He sat down and looked toward the sky. Clouds were arriving from the west and they were dark and growing larger. Buster guessed that the storm would break within 15 minutes or so. He started to breathe deeper, hoping for cool air to come along with the rain. Please, just a few minutes of fresh air, he thought. Let my stomach settle. There was a low growl of thunder in the distance. A few minutes passed and his son Dave opened the front door. "Dad? Feeling alright?"

"I will in a minute or two," Buster said.

"I don't think you're used to all that sugar," Dave said.

"Yeah," Buster said. "Your mom's been keeping me away from it. Yesterday she threw out our coupon book…the one from Jack's fundraiser." He sighed. "Can't remember the last time I had so much as a hamburger."

"She's just holding you accountable," Dave said. "She cares about you. We all do."

Buster looked up at his son and smiled faintly. "I know you do," he said. "And I'm lucky to still be here with ya."

"You've been doing great with the whole regimen," Dave said. "I can tell just by looking that you're healthier."

"You think so?"

"Oh yeah. I've really noticed it the past month or so. You just…you gained back some of that weight and you seem to have more energy." At that, Buster smiled. Dave sat down next to his dad, and they looked toward the sky and spent a minute in silence. The air was cooling down and a breeze tugged at the trees in the front yard. Flashes of lightning were veiled by the clouds above the horizon. "What did Dr. Assad say? Last time you were there," Dave asked.

"About my diet?"

"Yeah."

Buster paused, then said, "He just said to keep up with it. Same as before. Hopefully that means some good test results coming up here next month."

"I'd be shocked if they weren't good," Dave said. "You've really been on it lately."

"Well, I can never be too sure," Buster said. "Your sister was doing real good too before—"

"Dad. Dad, no," Dave interrupted. "You can't think like that. You can't. Anyway, Claire was just…too far gone by the time you started changing her diet. It just couldn't have happened."

"Mm. Maybe not," Buster said. "I could've done more, though."

"I don't know if it was up to you at that point," Dave said. Buster didn't respond. "She was just suffering for months on end," Dave continued. "I think it was her time."

"Maybe," Buster said. "I just wish I would've done something sooner."

Emma opened the door slightly and poked her head through. "Daddy?"

Dave glanced back. "Yes, hon?"

"What're you doing outside?"

"Pa-pa and I are just talking," Dave said.

"Is there gonna be a storm?" Emma asked. She looked at the sky from behind the screen door.

"Yep. Looks like it," Dave said. Emma opened the door and stepped out onto the porch. She sat on the edge of her dad's chair, and he put one arm around her as she watched the distant lightning.

"D'ya have a good birthday so far?" Buster asked.

Emma nodded. "Uh-huh."

"Can't believe you're already seven," Buster said. "You're growing too fast, just like your brothers did."

"Yeah, Aiden is already a teenager," Emma said, "and he thinks he's so cool."

"Your brothers think they're tough, huh?" Dave said. "They've got a little sis' so they want to act all grown up."

"Oh. I know," Emma said. She rolled her eyes and the other two laughed. They waited in silence as the storm clouds came in, a gray canopy unrolling across the sky. Muffled sounds of laughter were coming from inside the house. After a few minutes, Dave stood up slowly.

"I'm going to head back inside," he said. He patted Emma on the shoulder as she sat down in his place.

"Can I stay outside and watch?" she asked.

"Of course," Dave said. "Just stay on the porch with Pa-pa, alright?" Emma nodded and smiled. Dave turned toward the door. "Dad, do you need anything? Water? Seltzer?"

"I'll be fine, thanks," Buster said. He leaned back deeper into his chair. Emma sank into her own and sipped from a plastic cup full of juice. Dave closed the door behind him, and the conversation became muffled again. Buster sighed. "So, did you get everything you wanted?" he asked. "D'ya like your magazine?"

Emma nodded. "Yeah. It's my favorite," she said.

Buster smiled. He had bought her a subscription to National Geographic Kids. Dave had once told him that she had brought a dozen home from the school library. She read each of them, front to back, twice.

"Is it cloud-to-ground, Pa-pa?" Emma asked.

Buster paused. Once he understood the question, he said, "Oh, the lightning? I don't think so. Looks like it's just up in the clouds." Emma sipped her juice and sat back, looking upward as if she were at the movie theater. "You're not afraid of thunderstorms, are ya?" Buster asked.

Emma shook her head. "Not anymore," she said.

"Not anymore? How come?"

"One time, daddy let me sit outside and watch a storm with him."

"Ah," Buster said, "and you figured out they weren't so scary?" She nodded. "You know, when I was a real young kid—younger than you—I was terrified of thunderstorms," Buster said.

"You were?"

"Oh yeah. I couldn't fall asleep as long as there was a storm happening. Even when I'd run into my mom and dad's room. I just outgrew it, I guess. And I remember my mom always told me that thunder is just the angels going bowling in heaven."

"Really?"

"Really." Buster turned in his chair to face his granddaughter. "Have you ever heard of the 'calm before the storm'?" Emma shook her head. "Well," Buster said, "just wait now. Before the storm gets here, right before it starts to rain, the wind will stop. And everything will be real quiet."

Emma paused and looked at the sky, confused. "Why?" she asked.

"I'm not sure," Buster said. "I heard them talk about it on the Weather Channel before, but I forgot what they said."

"Was it the weathergirl? Payton?" Emma asked.

"Yep. I knew about it before that, but she just explained why it happens. Why it gets calm, I mean."

"Why does it?"

Buster shook his head. "I don't remember, sweetheart," he said. Emma looked to the sky again. She was silent and sat still for a minute. Buster watched her patiently and figured that she was listening for the calm. He looked west and listened with her.

"I wanna be a weathergirl," Emma said.

"Sorry, what'd you say?"

"I wanna be a weathergirl. They getta watch all the storms and make maps. And they know when it's going to rain and when it's gonna be sunny." She turned to face her grandpa. "Do you hafta go to college to be a weathergirl?" She rested her chin in her hand.

Buster chuckled. "Yes. I believe so," he said.

"If I go to college, I can be a weathergirl?"

"They'd have to call you a 'weather lady' by then," Buster said. "But yes. Of course you can."

Emma smiled. "Thanks, Pa-pa."

"You don't have to thank me," he said. He turned toward her again. "You know, when I was in high school, I wanted to be a meteorologist, too."

"What's that?"

"A weatherman."

"Oh."

"I had a whole collection of climate maps from all over the world. Hung 'em on the wall in my room. And I remember my grandma, your great-great-grandma, she bought me a Farmers' Almanac when I was thirteen. I read it a little bit, but I mostly just liked to go outside and watch when something was happening."

"Like right now?" Emma asked.

"Yep. Just like now."

"Why didn't you become a weatherman?" she asked.

"Well, I didn't go to college. My parents didn't have quite enough money," Buster said. "College costs a lot. Which I was pretty sad about."

"Can I still go one day? Like mom and dad."

"Yes. Yes, of course," he said. "You'll be able to go. I know you're going to. Your mom and dad have been saving money for you to go to college since the day you were born. Just like I did for your dad."

"So, I can go, too?" Emma asked. Her face was concerned.

"Yes."

"Promise?"

Buster looked at her. He put his hand on hers. "I promise,"

he said. "You'll be a great weather lady. Much better than the ones on TV now. You'll get the weather right. Every time."

"How do you know?"

"'Cause you're my granddaughter," Buster said. "And you're one smart cookie." He rustled her hair. She recoiled and started to giggle. They hadn't noticed that the rain was starting to fall. The thunder rumbled, low and unnoticed.

"Pa-pa?"

"Yes?"

"What would happen to me if I went out there? Would I get hit by lightning?"

"Probably not," Buster said. "But just in case, you shouldn't try." Emma didn't respond. Instead, she watched the rain fall. Each time she went silent, Buster could tell that she took in every sight and sound without distraction, pure and innocent. She was focused on something new and wouldn't speak a word. This time, it was the breaking storm. "You don't want to go back inside?" Buster asked. "You got a pile of presents in there that ya just opened." He hadn't finished talking yet before Emma started to shake her head. He felt as if he had interrupted her. She was caught in a reverie.

"Pa-pa?"

"Mmhmm?"

"Are you going to be here for Christmas this year?"

Buster thought, I hope so. I hope to God above. "Yes," he said aloud. "Yes, I'll be there."

"Mom said you were too sick last year."

"I was," Buster said. "Doctors said I had to stay at the hospital for a while. But I'm feeling much better now. In fact, your dad and I just talked about it. Don't ya think I look like I feel better?" He feigned a smile.

Emma stared at him and thought about it. "Will you be sick on Christmas again though?" she asked.

"I'm not going to let that happen," Buster said. "That's why I've been working hard to eat better and making sure I take my medicine." Emma asked him to promise that he'd be there at her house for Christmas and Buster promised it. "In fact," he said, "I'll make an extra box full of buckeyes and bring 'em just for you."

Emma smiled. "Thanks, Pa-pa."

"You're welcome," he said. He leaned toward her. "Now, you have to make me a promise." She nodded. "Don't let your brothers get any of those buckeyes," he said.

Emma smiled. "I promise," she said. "They don't need any more."

Buster laughed. "No, they don't."

The rain passed after 10 minutes and nothing was left but muted thunder. Birds began to chirp again, and the sky lightened to a brighter shade of gray. Sunlight broke through the clouds every few minutes. While the rest of the family left, Dave invited his father to stay for supper, and Buster accepted. He helped his daughter-in-law prepare utensils and plates as she put a shepherd's pie in the oven. In the corner of the living room, Emma sat in the middle of a tornado of running brothers. Her eyes were focused on the pages of National Geographic.

When supper was ready, Dave called out to Emma twice before she got up and came to the table. Buster's stomach felt better as they ate, but he worked at his meal slowly. He listened and laughed until everyone else had cleared their plate and was ready for a second helping.

It was 8 p.m. before Buster was ready to leave. Dave put two slices of cake in Tupperware and gave it to his dad. "I'm good with the cake," Buster said. "I'm sure your mom would like some, though."

"You know her well," Dave said. Buster thought of his wife waiting for him to return. He smiled. The family wished him well and said goodbye. Only Emma was missing. Buster looked around for her. "What happened to the little sugar cube?" he asked.

"She's out in the driveway," Dave said. He nodded toward the garage. Buster left with the cake and walked out toward his truck. Emma was at the edge of the driveway, standing in the grass. The rain fell in sprinkles. Emma's hand was over her eyes as she stared west.

"Whatcha looking for?" Buster asked.

"Rotation," she said.

"Rotation?"

"In case of a tornado," she said. "You never know."

"I guess you're right. Well, I better get home in that case. Thank you for the forecast, Miss Emma."

"You're welcome, Pa-pa." She realized he was leaving and

turned around. He gave her a hug and she mumbled some-thing. They let go of the hug and Buster leaned in closer.

"Say that again, hon."

"I said I'll find out why it gets calm before a storm hap-pens. Remember?"

"Of course. So, you'll find out? And you'll tell me why?"

"As soon as possible," Emma said. Buster smiled and got into his truck. As he backed the car out of the driveway, he waved to his granddaughter. She waved back and looked up at the sky once again.

The sun came out when Buster was halfway home. It was beginning to set, and it lit up the breaking clouds with colors of fire. Hopefully, he thought, Emma was able to see it, too. Buster remembered their conversation and knew that he wouldn't for-get about it. But part of him felt guilty. He second-guessed the truth of his promise about Christmas. But that was his only doubt. Everything else, he was most certain of.

Swimwear

HE WANDERED DOWN to the poolside around 7 a.m. because he could hardly sleep a minute, and the patio of the hotel mansion was quiet. No one else was around and there were only ruins of the night before. Half-empty glasses of champagne covered the tables where there had been groups of people standing and laughing with each other just hours before. The glasses looked like gold chandeliers in the glow of first light. The pool was completely still and there was little breeze. For a minute, the young man stood and breathed in slow and deep. He walked to the pool bar and sluggishly pulled himself up onto it, swinging his legs over so that he was inside. Then he used the fountain gun to pour a cup of lemonade. There were bottles of schnapps under the bar, but the young man wanted vodka. He tried to open the liquor cabinet and found that the door was locked. *I guess peach schnapps will do,* he thought. He poured half of a shot into the cup. A sunrise crested while the young man drank, and his lemonade-schnapps was lukewarm.

Birds chirped shyly in trees beyond the dark aluminum fence that walled in the pool. He leaned forward onto the bar and resisted the urge to nod off.

She walked up to stand by the edge of the pool, and he didn't notice her there until she began speaking. She held a phone up to her ear and talked just loud enough to be heard. He bit the inside of his cheek to make sure it wasn't a hallucination, and then he knew for sure that he was awake. She glanced over as he stared from under the string lights by the bar. The young man straightened his back. Her gaze locked onto him for a few seconds, and she suppressed a look of surprise. He avoided eye contact until the conversation wrapped up and she put down the phone. The birds were the only sound again.

"Hi, Jake." Madison's voice had not lost its honeyed shimmer. He held tighter to the cup. She continued, "I woke up and couldn't fall back asleep."

What are the chances? he thought. But he didn't say anything. There was a second of silence. Then he asked, "Did you have a good night last night?"

She nodded yes. "I met a lotta great people," she said. "I always wondered…is that what it's like to have Cameron as a best friend?"

"Yes," he said. "It's like having a hundred more friends I don't even know yet." She smiled, or at least, he thought that she did. His eyes were only a little less blurry.

"It's weird, isn't it?" she said.

"Well, he's your friend and my friend. I didn't expect him

24

to leave either one of us out."

"No, no. I just meant all the people he knows. I actually counted last night. There were fifty-eight people. Fifty-eight."

"If you hosted the thing, I bet fifty-eight thousand would've showed up," he said. She denied it, although they both knew she had just as many friends as Cameron. He let out a long sigh and said, "I can't even imagine the tab we all racked up."

"Yeah, I tried not to think about it," she said. "My guilty conscience couldn't take it, anyway."

The birds seemed louder now and the sky was growing pink. Jake hopped back across the bar to avoid feeling trapped. Madison stayed near the edge of the pool. She was wearing an olive sundress that she had on the night before. He knew that she couldn't have slept in it. "How's your summer been?" she asked. "Traveling a lot?"

"Yeah. It's been alright," he said. Then he confessed, "I hoped that last night was going to be the highlight of it."

She stared down at the pool and said, "Honestly, I was hoping so, too."

"It was a good night, though," he said. "I had a little too much fun with those guys from the skiing club."

"The ones that were buying the shots of Patrón?"

"Yeah," he said. "You met them, too?"

"I did," she said. "One of them tried to get me to hook up with him in the hot tub."

"What? Inside the hotel?"

"Yeah. I was like no, definitely not my thing."

"Which one was it?" he asked.

"I think his name was Brent."

"Ah," he said. He nodded and avoided eye contact. "Yeah, Brent was definitely the sketchy one."

"Oh, I know. I basically had to kick him to the curb."

"Good for you. You know, he had plenty of other options, anyway. That group of girls they knew followed them around all night."

"They did," she said. She looked up for a moment and met his eyes. He was familiar with the look on her face—it was as if all the life had drained from it and her eyes glossed over. Her voice softened. "Jake," she said. "Can I ask you something?"

He hesitated. Then he said, "Sure."

"Did you hook up with anyone last night?"

He set the cup down and folded his arms and shook his head. "I did not," he said.

"Oh. Okay. I just know that…well, you had a room to yourself and you seemed very social last night. I've never seen you like that."

He shrugged and said, "I was drunk."

"Hey, I've seen you drunk before. You never talked *that* much."

"Probably because I never drank tequila. Not back then."

"Oh, come on," she said. "It can't be just because of tequila."

He shrugged again. It wasn't clear to him what made him speak honestly, it could've been sleep deprivation or newfound maturity or both, but he said, "I've been getting out a lot lately. Drinking. Smoking. Socializing."

"I know."

"You do?"

"You post a lot on Instagram. You never did that before."

"Ah, yeah. That's true."

She glanced down at the pool again before speaking. "Do you miss me, Jake?"

He didn't want to look at the sadness in her face when he answered. "Maddy, you were my best friend," he said. "I've… yeah, I've missed you. I guess I've just been lonely and I'm trying to curb it."

"Oh. By drinking?"

He gave her a stern look. "I'm not an alcoholic," he said.

"I know you're responsible. It's just…a bender. But that's what it is, so I'm not gonna pretend it's not."

I already knew that, he thought. But he chose not to say it out loud. "Maybe it's too much," he said. "Especially because I know I did it to myself. I mean, I did it to us—to you."

She shrugged and said, "Well, yeah." He took a final gulp of the lemonade and threw away the cup. "Can we talk about it for a minute?" she asked.

"Sure."

"Promise me you'll tell me the truth."

"I promise. You know, I'm much better about it now."

"No boy is," she said, walking closer to him. "But actually, I will say it seems like you matured about ten years in two months."

"What do you want to know?" he said.

"How did this all come about?" she asked. "It just like… came out of nowhere."

Before he answered, he took in a deep breath. "It had been on my mind a while. A long while. I just thought it was commitment nervousness, you know. Something like that. But I thought about it enough and I knew that I couldn't try to change myself for you. Not that way. Even though I wanted to. And I tried to. I would've…lived a lie, basically. That wasn't fair to either one of us, most especially you, obviously."

"Okay, but what do you mean 'change'?"

"Change who I am. My spirituality. What I believe."

She nodded shyly. "I guess that makes sense. It was just so sudden. We didn't even have a chance to see each other or say goodbye."

"Yeah," he said. "And that's fair. I just couldn't keep it inside anymore." He scoffed. "You know, I've never been so tongue-tied and so anxious to say something at the exact same time."

"But over the phone?" she said. "I feel like I deserved better than that. I really did." He simply nodded. She sighed and said, "So much has changed, Jake." He said yes, he agreed, and he leaned back against the bar between two stools. It was silent and they both stared at the fiery horizon for a moment. A window in the turret of the hotel was open, and The 1975 was playing through it. He wondered if she heard it, too.

"You know you're still wearing your swim trunks?" she said. "Aren't you worried about getting a UTI?"

"Guess I didn't think about it," he said. "I left 'em on because was hoping to get up and go for a swim this morning. But obviously, that didn't happen." He sighed.

"Why?" she asked.

"Drank too much. Slept too little."

She looked up at him with caring eyes; asked, "Are you feeling alright?"

"Yeah, I am. All things considered."

"Mm. That's good."

"How are you? Have you had your first hangover yet?"

She shook her head. "I'm proud to say I haven't," she said.

"I find it hard to believe," he said. "I've seen you drink by the gallon before."

"I can sober up quickly," she said. "It's a little talent of mine."

"This is true. I've seen you in action before."

"You have. The many times I took care of you. Remember your birthday last year?"

"Yes," he said, trying to stifle a laugh. "I took a cold shower at 3 a.m. that night."

"And who made you drink water?" she asked. He smiled and playfully pointed at her. "Damn straight," she said. He realized that he was feeling comfortable in her presence, yet he didn't feel the energy to talk anymore. Meanwhile, The 1975 playing through the window changed to an older and slower song. She gestured toward the window. "Is that what I think it is?"

"It is," he said. "Wow. I was immediately reminded of fall 2016." They listened for a moment as the verse began. He looked at her and they both wore faint smiles. He extended his hand without thinking. She hesitated, then put her hand on his. He felt the familiar softness of it, not just her skin but the gentle way her hand wrapped around his. They came together and started to sway. He held her near to himself yet loose enough to feel comfortable. They looked separate ways but moved together slowly for a quiet minute.

"I know this song," she said. "What is it?"

"'Undo,'" he said. Whoever it was that was awake did not show themselves in the window, but the music continued at a low volume. Madison and Jake swayed together and held each other a little bit closer with each passing minute. He could feel the heat of her body radiating against his and heard her soft, easy breath.

"I miss this," she said. "I miss us."

"Me too," he whispered.

"We danced a lot," she said. "Especially last year, after ballroom. Wasn't it great?"

"I wouldn't've traded it for the world."

She smiled and said, "We got dang good at it, too. We even made Cameron jealous. And he's the ballroom king."

"Yeah. Or so he says."

She laughed. "Say what you want, but he taught you well." He smiled and they slowed to a standstill. Together, they stopped to lay down on a pool chair. She put her hand on his chest and he wrapped his arm around her, resting a hand on her shoulder. "Do you feel better?" she asked.

"Better? What about?"

"I don't know. It sounds weird, but I feel better. About you and me." She paused for a few seconds. "We're going to be alright. That's what I feel like."

He looked up at the sky and thought for a moment. "You know, I do feel better. I feel like we needed this to happen."

"Needed what to happen?"

"To see each other again," he said. "In the calm after the storm." She told him that she agreed. The rest of their conversation was unspoken. The music soon shifted to something pop, and a breeze made the palm leaves rustle above them. It became impossible to stay awake in the shared warmth, and Jake faded into sleep.

The air felt hotter and sunlight was filtering through the canvas umbrella as Jake woke up. He had one arm loosely wrapped around Madison's waist while she slept, and he was staring straight into her wavy, sun-bleached hair. Slowly, he rolled over onto the other edge of the chair and rose to his feet. Observing her for a minute, he wanted to lean over and kiss her forehead for the last time. But that would probably have woken her up, so he watched her silently and feigned a smile. Without looking back, he went upstairs and entered his hotel room. He took his wallet, keys, and phone out of his old backpack and put them inside a mini cooler he had brought. In the space that was left in the cooler, Jake shoved in the extra set of clothes that he packed. Then he threw the empty backpack away and carried the cooler with him to check out in the lobby. He waited patiently and tapped his foot on the floor while the concierge took back his room keys. Then Jake wished the man well before leaving directly through the lobby door.

There was a public park in front of the hotel that served as a corridor to the bay, and it was a gradual, treeless hill that sloped downward toward the water. Jake followed it down several hundred feet before walking onto an empty dock. At the end of it, he took off his shirt and shoes and removed the strings. He stuffed the clothing into the cooler and sealed it with the two latches. After he tested the cooler's buoyancy on the water, he took a shoestring and knotted it around the cooler's handle, then looped the other end around his ankle. It was the warmest hour of the day, and Jake started to feel hot flashes already. But he only waited for a second, breathing in deeply and stretching his back as if he had just woken up. Taking a look across the bay, he estimated and hoped that it was something short of a half-mile. Then he sprang forward off the end of the dock and made a flat dive into the gentle waves. With easy strokes, he began the swim and remembered what one of the ski club members had told him: there was a town on the other side of the bay with a street full of cantinas and a boatyard, and everyone who went there was only passing through.

April Snow

BAM! HE WAS DOWN—down like a dead oak in a windstorm. And now, Ty had to help him. The open pasture was alight with the crack of rifles and the drumming of machine guns, and it was all accumulating and crushing Ty's head like a vice. He focused on the task at hand in an attempt to ignore it. The boy knelt and unraveled the bandages from his canvas bag labeled with a marker-drawn red cross. "I need covering fire!" he yelled. Ty started to make a tourniquet for the fallen soldier, his brother by blood on the imaginary battlefield. The wounded brother grimaced and gripped his phantom bleeding shoulder. "Hold on, Sergeant Lee," Ty said. "Hold on." With a pained cry, the sergeant asked for morphine. Ty refused him. "We need you to get back out there!" he said. He finished the tourniquet and helped Lee to his feet. It took a minute as Lee found the strength return to his wobbling legs. Ty picked up the stick-gun from the ground and handed it to Lee and slapped him on his good shoulder. "Let's pretend they called a charge,"

33

he said quietly. Lee nodded. He turned sharply and aimed his gun forward. Ty took his stick-rifle and did the same. They looked at each other for a moment and turned toward the open pasture. Waves of viridescent grass flowed in the cold wind and the sky above was gray, and the two brothers watched as snow flurries carried with the wind across the battlefield. Ty raised his fist to the sky and Lee followed suit. Together, they kicked off the ground and burst into a most angry yell of "charge!" The brothers dashed through the waves of spring grass, stick-guns forward as if bayonets were attached. They raced down the hill toward the hordes of imaginary enemies cowering behind the embankment of the ravine.

"Hold the line!" Lee called out, waving on the rest of the infantry. They fought the sound of blaring guns as they grew closer and closer to the ravine and squinted their eyes to keep the wind and flurries from sending them into certain death. The brothers stopped at the very edge of the embankment and un-loaded their weapons into the ravine. Lee shouted and jumped into the bed of enemies, swinging his gun and jabbing with the invisible bayonet. He chopped at the tall blades of grass and tree roots, sending pieces of them into the air along with splash-es of creek water. Following him into the ravine, Ty noticed the shadow of a soldier running full-speed at his brother while his back was turned.

"Sergeant!" Ty called out. But he knew it was too late for Lee to help himself. Ty lunged toward his brother and swung his stick-rifle wildly at the enemy soldier. Lee turned in time to notice Ty's gun connect with a sapling and snap it in half. "You need to be more careful, Sarge," Ty said as he gasped for air.

The brothers decided to sit and relax, letting their backs rest against the embankment. Lee set his gun against a small stone. "Thanks for saving me, Corporal," he said. The brothers bumped fists.

"You're the energy and I'm the brains," Ty said. He held tight to his stick-gun. It was silent as they caught their breath and stared up toward the far edge of the pasture where the barbed-wire fence divided them from an empty cornfield.

Lee sighed. "I think I'm gonna head home," he said.

"Why?"

"I'm tired. We can come back tomorrow, anyway."

"We've only been here an hour."

"I know. I just don't feel like it."

"Do you want to work on a story later?"

"Maybe. I have homework."

"Are you serious? It's Saturday."

"You still can work on it if you want."

Ty scoffed. "Fine," he said.

Lee picked up his gun and straightened his safari hat. "Alright. See you later," he said. With crossed arms, Ty watched his brother leave the pasture and traverse the cornfield beyond the fence. Lee never glanced back, but Ty continued to watch. As soon as the former had crested the hill in the field, Ty hopped out of the ravine and gripped his stick-gun. He walked without any urgency now but found the energy to dream up another battle. There was an enemy sniper in the woods on the other side of the pasture. The bastard had shot down dozens of men. The captain called Ty forward and said he was the perfect sharpshooter to take him out.

"He won't get any more of us, Captain. I promise ya that," Ty said. He walked toward the wooded creek along a tree line where there were branches that draped far over the grass. He held his rifle half-heartedly and walked slowly. Once the boy was in the open field again, he had nearly forgotten the storyline of the sniper, his sharpshooting skills, and the raging battle.

Bam! Ty clutched his chest, imagining fresh blood flowing over his fingers. He stood for a second then fell to the ground, another victim of the sniper he failed to find and eliminate. The boy lay with one hand flat on the grass and the other on top of his heart. He thought of that girl from class, his wife, and how sad she would be to hear the news of his death. He took a deep breath and watched the gray sky in which he could see her lovely face looking down on him. He closed his eyes with that thought lingering and felt the silent, falling snowflakes brush against his face.

Nightwalk

A YOUNG MAN STEPS OUT of his apartment building and breathes in the cold city air. It's not as fresh as country air, but it's certainly fresher than the stale, oppressive air of his bedroom. A crisp emptiness is all around, and the streets are painted white with snow. The world outside is ill, but the outdoor air makes it seem more vigorous than any space confined by walls and doors or shuttered windows.

Walking uptown, the young man can count on one hand the number of passersby he sees. They're mostly couples, tightly entwined and talking only amongst themselves. Their mouths are masked and he cannot see them smile. Rich and soothing music pours from a few open windows among the high-rises. Vibrant life sits motionless in storefronts, made up of warm string lights and kaleidoscopic Christmas displays. But no people are indoors to enjoy them. Colorful lights explode among the trees and along the fences of a park—lush emerald greens, deep and fiery reds, and frosty icicle whites.

They sparkle in their reflection through the young man's glasses. He sees the display shift; the colors move in waves across the trees like a giant flag in the wind. Cool blue lights shimmer and move in silence. The trees are still and an ambiance of car tires on the pavement resounds across the snow. The young man walks to the center of the park where its separate walkways come together and spill into a circular garden. He sits down on a bench, resting inside the matrix of glittering lights. Farther down one of the walkways, an old couple is dancing, bathed in crystal white light. The young man turns to watch, careful not to stare. He can't hear any music, but the couple is there, swaying slowly and easily. A person walks by them without looking up and makes their way down the path and out of the park. And the old couple continues to dance. The young man smiles. He stares down at his shoes, but he smiles. As he looks back up, the couple stops and embraces. They hold each other for a moment. Then they walk leisurely, hand-in-hand, down the walkway and out of sight.

The park is silent and empty again as the young man stands up. He leaves the place behind and takes a different route back to his apartment, walking slower than he had before. At the door of his building, he stops and glances down the street toward the park. He smiles again. Then he opens the door and steps back inside to have a drink and listen to music while he lays on his bed and stares up at the golden string lights bordering his wall. Maybe, he thinks, he'll go for another walk tomorrow. And maybe the lights will still be there, still warm and sparkling. Maybe, in a month or so, he'll have someone to share them with—someone just as warm and just as vibrant.

Red Brick Hearts

JAE WAS MY ROOMMATE for half of a semester during our senior year of college, and we had known each other since we were 18. I had graduated and started working in central Ohio, and Jae stayed in school for his fifth year. He leased a house on the edge of Oxford, four blocks from uptown. So, I came down to visit him every chance I could, often three or four weekends in a row. I could not have gotten tired of it and never did. Jae was a good friend—sociable and selfless. And I would've gone insane being alone and bored in my apartment every weekend.

A warm May sun hung overhead the day before Jae's graduation. He and I left his house in the afternoon and walked east to uptown. He brought with us two Dominican cigars and a white lighter. I once told him that white lighters were bad luck, but he still carried one around. Uptown was quiet as we walked, or at least the part of it that was far from the big bars. The brick streets made an aesthetic rumble as cars passed, and people talked on the sidewalk in wispy conversation. Good weather brought more people out, but they kept to themselves, hiding behind hats and giant sunglasses. Jae seemed tired and he sighed several times as we took the sidewalk down High Street. He looked straight ahead. We didn't speak a word until we were at the bar patio and had bought two pitchers of beer. Everywhere there were barbacks and bartenders, and students came in and out of the open door with pitchers in their hands. "Too many people, yo," Jae said. He said we should ask someone to sit at their table. I told him that was all right, and so we joined a couple sitting in the corner. Jae took the barstool and I sat up on the banister. The beer was cold and flat, and I enjoyed it as the sun warmed my face. The guy sitting there had dark hair that was cut high and tight. He looked familiar and I hoped that he would recognize me and say something first. He was quiet but wore a smile and took a drink whenever we did. His girlfriend was blonde, tan, and freckled, and she immediately began to ask us questions. She sat with one foot on the stool in a half-squat, folding her arms across the table.

"Where are you from?" she asked Jae.

"New York."

"Gotcha. Are you Korean, by chance?"

Jae cleared his throat and said, "Yes." She said that was nice and that she and her boyfriend were from Indianapolis. Then I told her where I was from and that I had graduated a year before. "He's visiting me," Jae said. He put a hand on my shoulder.

"And my brother's graduating tomorrow," I added.

"Oh, that's fun," she said. "So am I." We talked about our majors and Miami and where we had lived during our four years there. She said that she was going to med school at Ohio State after graduation.

"Why do you want to go there?" Jae asked.

"Why not? They have the best programs there."

"Ohio's so shitty," Jae said. "Go to New York. Go to Boston."

She gasped. "Leave? Never," she said. She paused and looked down and stirred her mixed drink. "Well, you're sort of right. I was really hoping to get into UCLA." I asked her what happened. "Well, I got in," she said, "but moving to California just wasn't really practical." She continued stirring her drink.

"We're hoping to leave Ohio eventually, though," the boyfriend said.

"I would love to take a gap year, too," she said, "but that got shot down as soon as I decided on med school."

"You travel a lot?" I asked.

She nodded and looked up from her drink. "It would just be so perfect to take, like, a year off and live in Europe," she said. "I know so many people who've done that and just traveled all the time and made friends wherever they went. Ugh." She paused and counted on her fingers. "Let's see...where all have I traveled? I've been to Paris and Italy and Spain. But only for like a week. Which really isn't enough, you know? Not enough to get really immersed."

"Yo-o-o," Jae said. "People love going to Paris."

"Of course," she said.

"Why?"

"It's gorgeous."

"So is Prague," Jae said. "But no one wants to go there. Why?" He glanced at me and repeated it. "Why?"

"Hey, I'd go there," she said. "It's just not at the top of my list." She nodded in Jae's direction. "Why? Have you been to Prague?"

"Maybe," Jae said. "No one can prove it." I told her that he was there two weeks ago. There were posts tagged "Prague" on his social media. Jae laughed and denied it. He said that it wasn't him in the photos and that I needed to have my eyes checked.

The girl ignored Jae and asked, "Was it your first time?"

This time, he told the truth. "I've been there ten times," he said.

"Ten times! Why?"

"So many good clubs to go to," he said. "And good people. Some people will take out their card and buy a hundred drinks for everyone there. Someone gives you a shot and says, 'Here, take this. It's free.'" I wondered for a second if he knew a woman in Prague. He used to know two in the UK and made multiple trips there during the year. Jae had sent all of our roommates a picture of him lying next to one in bed. Then he denied that it ever happened each time we brought it up.

"So, how have you been to Prague ten times?" the girl

continued. "Do you just go for the weekend or something?"

"Usually," Jae said.

"That's crazy. Aren't your flights really expensive?"

"Sometimes."

I explained to her that Jae and I were roommates when we lived uptown. "He'd leave the three of us for like a week. Unannounced," I said. "He'd just disappear and then we'd see pictures of Prague or Singapore or something on his Instagram story."

"Seriously?" she laughed. Then she turned to Jae. "You could just leave like that and spend a week in Europe?"

"Sometimes just three days," Jae said.

"Still. I couldn't handle traveling that much."

"It sucks sometimes," Jae said. I told him not to complain—traveling a lot was a good problem to have. He put a hand on my shoulder and said, "You have no idea, boy."

Later, Jae cut the cigars and explained to the couple how his friend gave them to him at a club in Amsterdam. The friend's dad owned a cigar company in Santiago, and he was spending half a year abroad. We lit them and started puffing, and I held the smoke on my tongue like Jae always told me to. The smoke was not sweet, but it was rich and it went in smoothly. We were the only people on the patio smoking cigars. The girl and I asked Jae more about his travel stories and women he was seeing, but he dismissed it all with "a gentleman never tells." We laughed in his face and continued questioning. After a few minutes, he tried to change the subject and joked and said that Americans have a traveling obsession. I told him that he wasn't any better than us. "Right? And besides, I'm from the Midwest," the girl added. "What else am I supposed to do for fun?"

The conversation lulled, so I finished the last of the beer and sent a text to my brother. He had said he would join us uptown around 3:00. I asked the guy if he had also graduated and he said that he would be graduating on Sunday with the rest of them. There was a pause and we both looked at each other; hesitated. I asked if he knew Cameron Hastings. He said he didn't. Then he paused, thought about it, and said, "You look familiar, though." He asked if I knew Connor and then I realized we had met at a party at his house.

"Yeah, yeah," I said. "Connor's my brother. I think we've met before."

"I've seen you around his place a couple times," he said. He told me he was in ROTC with Connor and that he was a good guy and he hoped he would get a nice job somewhere. I told him Connor was hoping to be assigned infantry. "Ah. That's where I wanted to be, originally," the guy said. "I'm hoping for armored now."

"Why's that?"

"I heard a lot of good things from some guys who went armored," he said. "It sounded like it was more my speed. Plus, I like tanks."

"Hopefully it works out for you," I said.

"Thanks. Yeah, hopefully."

It was just after 3:00 and the bar was even more crowded. We were almost shoulder-to-shoulder now. Connor walked onto the patio with one of his roommates and two ROTC sophomores named Ryan and Sarah. They stood near us along the banister. Connor asked how long we had been there. I said an hour. He nodded and picked up the rest of my cigar and started to light it. "Is this yours?" he asked.

"Yeah," I said. "Jae bought them."

"They look expensive."

"They didn't cost," Jae said. Connor nodded and started to puff the cigar. Sarah, Ryan, and Connor shared a laugh over the other guy for being hungover at their last ROTC function, and he laughed with them, and they shared rumors about other cadets and which of them they hated most. Jae and I listened and he gave me his pitcher, so I drank what was left of it. We got up after a minute to let Connor's friends sit down, and Jae and I stood against the banister next to Connor. We kept our voices low.

Connor asked, "So, how'd you meet Jack?"

I pointed to Jae. "It was packed in here, so he said we should ask to sit with 'em," I said. "I had no idea who they were, but then we got to talking."

"Nice."

"They're both cool," I said. "We had a good conversation."

"Yeah, they're nice. His girlfriend is pretty chill," Connor said. I told him yes, I agreed. Then Connor turned to face Jae and said, "How are you doing, man?"

"I'm good, yo."

"Are you still living in Oxford?"

"For one more week."

"I heard you have a thousand-dollar bottle of wine in your house."

Jae laughed. "Ahh," he said. "That's only a rumor." I laughed because I knew it was true. He had bought it in Europe for graduation. Jae stored wine bottles in most of his cabinets and his refrigerator and on the fireplace mantle. He never drank them, only gave them away.

Connor continued and asked Jae if he'd been on any trips recently, so Jae told him that he went to Prague and London and had a nice time. He didn't mention any other details. Connor turned to me and asked, "Speaking of which, did mom and dad tell you about Georgia?"

"No."

"I don't think they can swing it."

"Why's that?"

"Timing. Plus, dad's car still needs fixed."

"Ah," I said. "Well, that sucks. Maybe later this year, though. I'm not sure I would've been able to fly out to begin with."

"Yeah, no worries," Connor said. "Save up some money. I don't know what my timeline is after BOLC, but we'll see."

"Hopefully we can make it happen," I said. Meanwhile, Jae stood next to me and stayed silent. He usually did so in groups of more than four people. Connor and I shared the rest of the cigar until it tasted too bitter. I stamped it out and we sipped beer to wash down the taste of smoke. I wanted to bother Cameron about joining us in Oxford, so Jae and I sent him videos of us on the bar patio. He responded immediately and said that he'd be in town later that night. I told him that we'd be waiting there.

When it was close to 5:00, the conversation slowed down. Ryan asked if anyone had a deck of cards, but no one did. Connor suggested that we go to his house and relax for a few hours. "Before tonight?" I asked. He nodded. Then Jae said that he was going home to take a nap, so I told him to text me and we would meet later.

"I don't know if I'll still be here, yo," he said.

"You will be," I said. But I wasn't completely sure. We shook hands and then I stepped off the patio, following just behind Connor, Ryan, and Sarah. The sound of the bar faded after we crossed the street toward Poplar. There was a lush wall of shade along the sidewalk as we walked downhill. The sun shined in the west and was splintered by the trees. Connor was texting and he didn't look up, but I could hear him singing low—a Bob Marley song. I smiled. It made me feel sad that we wouldn't be going to Georgia in June, but I didn't think about it again after we left the bar. It was warm outside and too good of a day.

Above the Grapevine

WHEN I WAS 21, I started a job as a busboy at the Starlight. I had never worked a restaurant job before, and I had never been to Tier Two, which was the home of the Starlight and many other wealthy clubs that were too many to count. At the time, I lived on Tier Four which was about 50 levels below Tier Two, and it was where urban congestion was the thickest. Tier Four only saw the sun during the two hours around noon, and no snow made it down there in the winter. Tier Three saw a few more hours of light and a few flurries of snow, but Tier Two was close enough to the Top that they saw the sun in the day and had small pockets of snow in the winter. Decembers at the Starlight quickly became my favorite time of the year.

A tram ran from Tier Four up to Tier Three, and I would get on it every day to get to work. It was always full when I made it on, and I had to stand most days, but the ride only cost 75 cents. The tram would cruise through the dark spaces of Tier Four for about 15 minutes and stop at a packed station just below Tier Three. I'd get off there and take a public stair-well that led up to the next tier. Then I went through a small skybridge after getting off the stairs, and the skybridge led to an elevator hub. One of the elevators there went up to Tier Two. Once at Tier Two, I went through another skybridge to a public lobby where there were fountains in the four corners of the room and marble floors, and most people there sat around wearing suits. A series of two skybridges left from the lobby, and the two were connected in the middle by a terrace that featured some sodded grass and a handful of shrubs. The second of the bridges led directly to the back door of the Starlight. It took me 30 minutes to get to work every day. Sometimes it was 40. Near the entrance of the Starlight was another tram, and it ran almost twice as fast as the one on Tier Four. But the faster tram was only accessible to the top couple of tiers. Starlight regulars and VIPs would often step off that tram, already with a drink in their hand and buttoning their blazers and laughing loudly. The management team gave me a set of three keys when I started at the club. One of the keys unlocked the skybridge that entered the elevator hub. It was the only key I had that gave me access anywhere above Tier Three. The other two keys unlocked the Starlight's liquor cabinet and the cooler behind the kitchen. I used all three keys on a daily basis.

By the time I marked six months on the job, fall had fizzled to its end. The club members began to come in with thicker jackets. The walls and hallways of the Starlight shifted from autumn décor to glittery fake snow and bright Christmas ornaments. Summer and fall were hot and sticky for any tier below the Top, so winter brought more high-tier people to the Starlight and they seemed to smile more and talk louder then. The rest of us felt it, too.

The first Saturday of December, I had a towel in my back pocket before I even stepped into the clubhouse. I had left work just 10 hours before and forgot to put the towel in the hamper. It was my third double shift of the week. Jenn was bent over the computer and glanced over as I clocked in. She had dark hair that was about three feet long, and she always put it up for work. Altogether, it was the size of a rose bush. "Hey Cole," she said. I said hi to her and then checked the reservation schedule. There were 20 dinners and they all began between 5:00 and 6:00. "I'm going to need a weekend after this weekend," Jenn said.

"How many doubles have you worked?"

"Four."

"Whoa."

"Yeah." She grabbed a pen from behind the reservation book. "By the way, Howard is looking for you."

"Why, what's up?"

"I don't know," she said. "He's running a hundred miles an hour." I nodded and turned to find Howard before he could run into me and knock me over. Two of our bartenders were at the tavern in the center of the club. One was at the left end and one was at the right end. They were stacking clean glasses and loading the fridge with beer. At the other end of the tavern,

Howard appeared in the doorway, pointing toward the center of the floor. My friends Chris and Brian entered. They were carrying a table and set it down where Howard was pointing.

"Careful," he said. His voice was always a low shout and he enunciated each word. "We're going to have two more tables," he said. "Set both of them for five. Five. Then come see me. Alright?"

"Alright," the boys said. Howard turned on his heel to leave. Then he looked up and saw me standing there.

"Hey, big guy. How are you?"

"Good."

"I was looking for you."

"Yeah. I had a double today, so I got back at four."

"Okay," Howard said. He nodded and put both hands on his hips and glanced around the room. "We're going to need a banquet table at the end here. I'll send the other boys to get it." He looked back at me. "You know where the tablecloths are?"

"Yes."

"Down by the liquor cabinet? Where all the plastic cups and plates are."

I nodded. "Yeah."

"Okay. We need three white squares and one long. Okay? The long goes on the banquet table, once they get it up. The squares go on these three here." He pointed at the tables and glanced back to make sure I saw them. "And if you can grab some bread-and-butter plates after that, we'll get this show on the road. Alright?"

"Sounds good."

"Go ahead now," Howard said. He had done an about-face before I finished nodding and turned toward the hallway. Then I raced down the stairs and grabbed the tablecloths. Moving too quickly, I dropped one. I snatched it from the floor and went back up the stairs. We had less than one hour to get the banquet set up. Chris and Brian were in the middle of the dining room and snapping open the legs of the table.

"There he is," Brian said.

"Here I am." I tossed the tablecloth on Chris's shoulder.

"Yo." He glanced at the tablecloth. "You trying to do some work around here?" he said.

"I could use a shot first," I said.

"Huh, well if you're up for it, there's like four bottles by the bar," Brian said.

"I'll wait 'til the members get here," I said. "Then I'll really need it." I put the tablecloths on the three dinner tables, then Chris, Brian, and I finished setting up the plates and the banquet table and made sure the food was covered. It was 4:45. We sat down on the window sill. Occasionally, we glanced toward the double doors in case Howard came crashing in.

"I don't smell, do I?" Chris said.

"No," I said. "Why?" He pinched his thumb and index finger together and brought it up to his pursed lips, pretending to inhale. Meanwhile, Brian was staring at the rows of food. "Ahh," I said. "You do that on the way here?"

"Right before I leave, actually," Chris said. "Gives me

time to cover the smell."

I joked, "You might want to open your eyes a little wider, though."

Chris looked at me nervously. His eye twitched. "Seriously?" he asked.

"No, you're good."

"Damn, dude. Don't make me paranoid like that."

"You think Howard ever smokes?" Brian asked.

"Nah," I said.

"I bet he does that booger sugar, though," Chris said.

"He has to," Brian said. "Dude zips around like a bullet train."

Suddenly, Sylvia flung the kitchen door open and clapped her hands in our direction. She was in her 50s and was the oldest server at the club. "You boys better not let Howard catch ya like that," she said. "Not on Guest Night. He's already gotten on the doorboys about setting up the entrance."

We got down from the window sill and tucked our towels in our pockets. "He only gets mad at the men," Chris muttered.

"We're standing guard here," I explained.

Sylvia scoffed. "Guarding the food?" she said. "You'll be lucky to get any of that tonight. I'll be taking three boxes home. At least." She stood in front of us and put a defiant hand on the banquet table. Brian leaned over the table and grabbed a piece of chicken and popped it in his mouth. He smiled as he chewed, and Sylvia smacked him on the arm. "Brian! You're about to get Howard on all of us right now. And I ain't going down with you." She turned back toward the kitchen door. "Help us water the tables," she said without glancing back. Brian was still smiling as we walked into the kitchen. We filled two pitchers each with water and started to pour the glasses. We began at the dining room left of the bar and worked our way to the right. Howard did loops around the tables in the room. He was talking randomly but I wasn't listening. A few members were walking in early as we poured water. They hung their coats in the closet then rubbed their hands together and their eyes were focused on the bar. The first group was a pair of married couples. I recognized two of them as the Schottensteins. Once the club was eventually full, I would look around and notice that I only knew half of the faces in the crowd. That was how Guest Night turned out every year.

Nathan was the only bartender in the room then and he stood ready to serve, but I saw his eyes look up and down at the group. The outfits were always the highlight of any event for him. I put one hand on the bar and set the empty pitcher down next to him. Janet Schottenstein was walking down the hall with a woman who was wearing a cocktail dress that had a pattern of gold and green. Nathan described it as martini-olive green. "Her guest needs to get a clue," he said. "Get real. I mean, that dress looks like it's been in her closet for forty years."

"Forty years and forty extra pounds," I said.

Nathan shook his head. "You're worse than I am," he said. I laughed and went back to watering the tables. More groups came in and I was waiting behind the bar with Chris and Brian, our hands clasped behind our backs like true busboys. After a minute, Howard came rushing by. He snapped his fingers at us and through pursed lips, he told one of us to get the fuck out there and greet people. His face reddened and then he darted off.

"That's the doorboys' job," Brian muttered. He crossed toward the atrium and started saying "Hello, sir" and "How are you, ma'am?" Chris and I decided to loiter around because we wouldn't have the opportunity in the following hours. We went in opposite directions. That was the busboy tactic for avoiding Howard. He could only snap at us one at a time. So, I went down the hall and opened the double doors at the entrance where the two doorboys were sitting inside. Through another set of doors were a brick patio and a small courtyard that led to the tracks. Trams cruised by and they were a silver blur. One of the doorboys there was my age. The other was 17. The servers referred to him as Al, but all of the guys called him Finker. It had a condescending ring to it, but I still liked Finker. Most of us did. Every guy working at the Starlight was called by his last name anyway. Howard was the only one who didn't abide. I firmly believed that he didn't know my name. Still, I decided to work for him three years in a row.

"We're taking bets," I said to the doorboys. "How many Tier Four guests you think'll be coming tonight?"

"How d'we know they're from Tier Four?" Finker asked.

"If they have more than one tattoo."

"Fair enough. I'll say—I don't know—twenty."

"Oh yikes," I said.

"Too low?" Finker asked.

"I bet thirty-two," I said. "Because, you know, you gotta account for couples."

Finker nodded. He looked up, thinking. "Here's a better bet," he said. "How many of 'em you think will get piss drunk?"

"If they're from Tier Four? That'd be all of them."

Finker laughed. "Fair enough," he said. "Alright, I'll say thirty-three," he decided.

"Final answer?"

"Yes," he said. So, I collected two bucks from him and left the entranceway. More people were starting to come through now. I pegged one of them as a Tier Four guest. He was wearing brown loafers and a pair of old slacks. Most club members had boat shoes or chukka boots, and they liked to wear tight golf pants.

As soon as I had left the entrance, Howard came by and put a hand on my shoulder. "Let's get the buffet set up, alright?" he said. I told him I would and he flew away. Chris, Brian, and I went into the kitchen and began hauling the food out to the table in the middle of the dining room. Each time we went back for a new dish, more people appeared in the clubhouse. We had to navigate between clusters of people now, and there was hardly an open space throughout the dining room. Chris and I stood guard at the buffet table with our hands folded behind our backs. People were sitting down and eating, and some were at the bar. Nathan darted back and forth behind the bar as he mixed drinks. He would be making the same set of motions for the next six hours.

"I got sixteen so far," Chris said.

"What? Oh, the bet," I said. "I've only seen fourteen."

"Dr. Trenton brought a couple of guys with him. They were smoking on the deck a little bit ago, wearing jeans."

"Was one of them his son?"

"What's his son look like?"

"Bald. Long nose. They come for dinner every Thursday and he's always going out to the deck to smoke. I swear he goes through a whole pack every night."

"Hm. Actually, I think it was him."

"Okay, well, he doesn't count," I said. "His son lives up here but he belongs on Tier Four. He's unemployed and his dad just takes him everywhere and pays for it."

Chris scoffed. "Nice. Wish I had a dad like that."

As the clubhouse filled to its maximum, dinner continued. The busboy crew and I rushed around to fill water glasses and clear tables for a good two hours until mealtime ended. It phased into drink time and people surrounded the bar, appearing to smother Nathan and the other bartenders. I cleared the last few tables, passing by a handful of members. Our greetings were always the same: "Hi, Cole. How are ya?" "Mr. Harris! Good to see you." "Well, hello, Cole." "Hi, Mrs. Walker. How're you doing?" "Packed house today, huh?" Then I'd laugh and say "yes, ma'am" and leave toward the kitchen.

Within a few minutes, everyone had a drink in their

hand and the dining room tables were cleared. We reached the mid-evening lull. Chris, Brian, and I met in the kitchen for just a minute before we scattered. If Howard found us together, we'd have a mountain of sidework to do. I decided to visit the doorboys again. As I walked up to the entranceway, I saw Finker between the doors. He was standing and talking to a short, brown-haired girl. She looked like she was in her early 20s, and she wore a loose navy dress. Finker said something and she laughed. The corners of her mouth turned up as she smiled, and her eyes fell into a soft droop. I opened the door. "Hey, Browning," Finker said. "Do you know where the ladies' locker room is? I have no idea." The girl's hands held tight to a purse. There was a dark stain on the right side of her dress. She looked at me; saw that I noticed the stain. Her couldn't-help-it smirk suggested that it was wine. Finker looked at me again. "Browning?" he said.

"Yeah."

"I just asked you where the ladies' locker room is."

"Yeah," I said. "Yeah. It's downstairs. But you've gotta go through the side hallway."

"Oh," the girl said. "I'm—I'm not really sure where that is. I'm just a guest of the Schottensteins. They don't work out here, so they don't know where it is either." I looked at her. She kept her eyes on mine.

"Ah, okay. You know what?" I said. "I'll just walk you down there."

"Will you? That'd be great." Her voice was milky, relaxed.

I led the both of us out of the entranceway toward the ball-room and then down the stairs. We were silent for about 30 seconds. My cheeks began to feel warm. I rushed to think of something to say.

"So, how do you know the Schottensteins?" I asked.

"Oh, well. My mom worked for their restaurants for about twenty years. She managed a couple of 'em and I guess they just got pretty close. I mean, I don't know them super well, my-self. But it's nice that they're friends."

"So, you've been here before?"

"A few times," she said.

"Where do you live?"

"Tier Four. By the market district."

I laughed, "You're kidding."

"Not at all," she said. I stopped at the bottom of the stairs and looked at her. She wasn't smiling.

"I'm sorry. I didn't think you were serious," I said. Most people I knew in my neighborhood didn't have her sense of style, her soft features, or her friendliness. I didn't say that, how-ever. I said, "You just…don't put off a Tier Four vibe. But that's not a bad thing."

"I get it. Don't be sorry," she said. She laughed and con-tinued, "I'm guessing you're from Tier Four, too."

"Yeah. I am. I'm a few blocks from the market district and like one level down. Most people there are pretty dumpy. Solid threes, I'd say." She laughed and that made me smile.

"I know what you mean," she said. "Just spending a couple hours with the Schottensteins up here makes everybody under Tier Three look like a…"

"…A mutant?"

"Yeah. Pretty much."

"I can see that," I said. "Just from working here."

"You know, you don't seem like you're from Tier Four either," she said.

"Thanks," I said. "I guess that's the new compliment now."

"What'd you mean?"

"Telling someone: 'You know, you don't look like you're from Tier Four.'"

She laughed again. "Oh yeah, I like it," she said. "That should be it."

I glanced behind me. "Sorry, I forgot why we were here," I said. "The locker room is down that hallway. The carpeted one. Third door on the right."

"Right," she said. "Thank you." She walked toward the doorway into the hall and then turned around. "By the way, I don't think I said my name. I'm Sandra."

I nodded in her direction and said, "Nice to meet you. I'm Cole."

"Maybe we'll see you around, Cole," she said. It sounded uncertain, like a question.

I pretended to glance at my watch and joked, "Well I'm here until ten, so I don't really have a choice." Sandra smiled at that and I smiled back. Then she turned down the hallway and disappeared around the corner. I flew up the stairs, taking them two at a time.

Guest Night rolled along and I was too busy to think about anything else. Tables were filling and refilling with empty glasses, plates, and silverware. I broke two wine glasses early in the night. They shattered across the kitchen floor, and all of the line cooks clapped sarcastically. I wanted to slow down after that, but we couldn't. We could only try to be more careful. The doorboys sat in their furnished room until Howard recruited them to clear tables and refill the buffet food. They stuck out among the crowd, walking slowly while the other busboys and I pinballed around the room in a near-jog. Brian shook his head and made an exasperated sigh every time I passed him in the kitchen. Chris was serious, never glancing at me unless I asked him something. He put his head down and cleared three tables by himself in just two minutes.

It was 6:00 when the busyness peaked. We cleared tables as quickly as possible so that we could have a minute or two to take a break and talk. Chris and I took a couple of swigs of the amaretto in the back bar. Sylvia rounded the bar and snatched the bottle from Chris. "Gimme that! You want the members to see ya doing that? Or worse, Howard?"

"They're too drunk to notice," Chris said.

"Howard'll fire you for that," Sylvia said. She put the cap back on the bottle and returned it to the shelf.

"Yeah, right. He'd have to fire everyone then," Chris said. He leaned against the back wall. My eyes drifted over the ballroom full of faces. At a table in the right corner, Sandra was sitting with the Schottensteins and the Martins. Mr. and Mrs. Martin sat forward with their arms crossed over the table. Sandra's right side faced me and she held a glass of wine close to her chest. She was leaning back in her chair, listening. After a moment, she tucked a strand of hair behind her ear. She glanced toward the bar, so I held my gaze and she found me there. For a second, we looked at each other. She turned away; smiled.

Later, Chris and I began to move back and forth through the hallway to look busy. As I turned out of the kitchen empty-handed, Howard stopped me. "Hey, big guy. What time d'ya come in today?" I told him 10:00. "So, you're working a double," he said. "Didn't realize we had so many damn doubles today. Tell you what—it's dying down and we got plenty of servers in there. You can clock out at seven if you want."

"Thank you."

"Okay," he said. "We'll see you tomorrow." He turned to leave and I didn't hesitate. It was two minutes 'til seven when I entered the ballroom and cleared one last table and dropped off the glasses in the kitchen. Chris shook his head and sighed as I punched out. I just laughed and opened the outside door. Then I stepped out onto the loading area and took a breath of the cold air. Around the corner, I heard the juvenile laughs of doorboys hanging around the entrance. I decided to join them. They were laughing a lot and I was hoping that Sandra might pass through again. I climbed the stairs while zipping up my coat. Alvarez and Finker were standing up against the wall and out of view of the doorway.

"You son of a bitch," Alvarez said. "Did you just get off?"

"Yeah," I said. "Why are you guys still here?"

"We have to stay for when everyone leaves tonight," Alvarez said. "It's one of those events."

"Gotcha. Hospitality on steroids."

"Basically," Finker said. Alvarez took out a cigarette and lit it. I asked him what the hell he was doing.

He said, "Eh, no one's coming out for a while." A few seconds later, we were talking and the inside door opened. Someone was crossing through the foyer. Alvarez dropped the cigarette, stomped on it, and kicked it toward the gutter. Finker opened the outside door and then Sandra stepped outside.

"Thanks," she said. "Oh hey, Cole."

"Hey."

She asked me if I was off, so I told her yes. "Oh, good," she said. "Do you mind helping me with something?" Behind her, I could see Alvarez winking at me. I pretended I didn't see him. I told Sandra sure. She said that she had to run something home and wondered if I'd go along with her.

"Of course," I said. Alvarez and Finker were both smirking at each other as they headed for the door. I turned away and followed Sandra down the stairs, through the dark courtyard, and into the tram. We sat and she turned to me.

"Thanks," she said. "I gotta be honest…I just wanted to get out of there. I don't actually have to run anything home."

"Don't apologize," I said. "We've all been there." She

asked how my night was and I told her how days went as a busboy. Meanwhile, the outside lights streaked by, sharp and glowing from the darkness beyond the window. She listened to me and nodded and smiled as I rambled. Ten minutes passed before I realized we were going up and not homeward to Tier Four. "Is this Tier Two?" I asked. "Where are we?"

"We're near the top of Tier Two," Sandra said. "I was wondering if you wanted to see something with me."

"See what?"

"Well, I have a key to the Top Tier that Mr. Schottenstein gave me a while ago. I love going up there in the winter. And in the summer when the sun sets. I thought you might like it, too."

"You mean we're going up to the Top?" I asked.

"You've never been there?"

"Never," I said. Suddenly, I wondered how it would go. Would someone up there see I was from Tier Four? And what was the rule for letting people in? I didn't say anything though, not wanting to ruin the opportunity. We got off the tram inside a bright room where a white marble floor unfolded in front of us. It was lined by tall, stark columns and a flowery-designed ceiling several feet overhead. I craned my neck to look up at it, but only for a second. I didn't want to trip and fall into Sandra.

"This is the lower station," she said. "It's close to the Schottenstein's cottage." She held up a bronze key. It looked almost exactly like my own apartment key. "This goes to a stairway that pops out pretty close to their yard," she said.

"They have a yard?" I asked.

"Of course," Sandra said. "I mean, the cottage is at the Top. So it'd be a waste if they didn't have a yard." We turned a few corners in the marble station. It was silent and so empty that it was unsettling. Only one man passed by, wearing a suit and looking straight ahead. He nodded in our direction, but he said nothing and we said nothing. Sandra stopped in front of a door which was the middle in a row of three. She unlocked it and we headed up a set of stairs the same white marble as the station. At the top, I opened the door for her. We were greeted with a rush of cold air, and I immediately smelled something unfamiliar. It was pleasant and nearly sweet, kind of like the smell I'd get walking by fresh vegetables at the market. There was a sidewalk ahead of us, and it was lined by an endless row of trees and warm, yellow streetlamps. As snowflakes fell, they captured the light and fell to the ground like glitter.

"God, I've never seen so many trees in one place," I said. "Are they real?"

"I think so," Sandra said. She plucked a dead leaf from the nearest branch and let it go so that it floated down slowly with the snow. We walked forward and the line of trees ended and there was a fork in the sidewalk. Sandra went to the left and I followed her. Ahead of us, the streetlamps were growing farther apart, and beyond them, I couldn't see anything. Sandra took another left and then there were no more streetlamps. I hesitated before following her into the darkness. "It's okay, I know where I'm going," she said. We walked farther and now the light was behind us. I saw a few faint lights in the distance, but everywhere else was darkness—nothing. After a minute, I could start to make out the falling snow. Then I looked up and around. There was a layer of snow everywhere. A blanket of shadowed whiteness extended into eternity on every side of us. Looking up, I saw a pale orange color covering the entire expanse of the sky. It went all the way from behind us to in front of us and from left to right, kissing the white blanket of snow at each horizon. In front of us, little white lights were coming from some dark structure that sat above the snow. I kept looking around while we walked, feeling small and suddenly vulnerable. But still, I couldn't look away and wondered just what the hell I had been missing my entire life.

We reached the cottage and sat down on the stoop. Sandra already had a coat, but I offered her mine anyway. She said I was sweet, but she declined. We moved closer to each other and then we were warm. I saw a few figures pass on the sidewalk, quiet silhouettes walking through the falling snow. Sandra told me about where she grew up and the high school she went to, which had played against my high school at least once a year. She said that her mom grew up with the Schottensteins there, and when Mr. Schottenstein's first restaurant took off and he started to build more of them, he told Sandra's mother that he knew he'd have a trustworthy manager to hire. Unfortunately, Sandra said, managers only make Tier Four kind of money and the man with the brilliant idea got all the rest. So, she was allowed to visit the top two tiers when it was appropriate, but the rest of the time, she lived in the dirty, noisy, and crowded lower tiers with the rest of us. I told her it was all right though because she grew up well and had class. "You don't need money for that," I said. "That's one thing I've learned at the Starlight."

"Don't need money to be happy either, but it really helps," she said.

"Do you really think that?" I asked.

"A little bit, yeah," she said. "But not that it's ever bothered me. I just think it's funny to hear people say that because we all know there's a little bit of truth to it." She looked up at the sky and sighed. "I used to want that kind of life, you know. The Schottensteins are good people, really, but you see some of the people they run around with, the people who live up here—" She gestured at the land around us. "—and you see how they act. They're no better than most of the people on Tier Four or Tier Five. They just have the money to misbehave more often now. You've probably seen some of them at their worst."

I said yes, and I had heard some of their worst, too. Every drunken tale of divorce and estranged kids and addiction. "I think you're right," I said. "But still, I just wonder sometimes what it's like."

"I'm okay with not really knowing," Sandra said.

"Well, I admire you," I said.

She thanked me and asked, "So, what do you think?"

"About the Top Tier? I can't believe people really live here, with all this room and the sky overhead. And the weather." I pointed behind us and asked, "Is this really the Schottenstein's cottage? Matt and Janet Schottenstein?"

She nodded. "And I think Dr. Rimer also lives near here," she said. I didn't say anything and just shook my head. She smiled and said, "Exactly what I thought, too." I watched her as we sat there and she kept her eyes on the sky. The breeze tossed up the ends of her hair and snow flurries fell on it and made a lovely pale glitter. "Nights like this almost make it worth it," she said. I asked her what she meant, but she shushed me and said that I was ruining the moment. Inside, I was dying to tell her that she was the most beautiful girl I'd ever seen. But instead, I shut my mouth and felt the snowflakes sting my face. I laughed when one got in my eye, then she laughed too. We kissed and our faces were numb, but I could still feel her warm, soft lips. We sat in the cold air and didn't feel the need to talk. The snow became lighter and thinner, and so we decided to walk back to the tram. I had almost forgotten there were four other tiers below us. We couldn't hear them from the Top, and I was startled when we got back into the tram and it screeched and hollered as it rushed away from the station. We got off at Tier Two and changed trams, then switched once again at Tier Three. As the third tram pulled away, Sandra asked if she'd see me again. I was hoping that she would ask. I told her I'd be at the Starlight again the next day and every Friday through Wednesday. "We'll have to do something like this again," she said.

"Yes," I said. "Yes, we will. I'd love to." Minutes later, we were back at Tier Four, and I could already sense that it was darker outside the tram. Sandra got off at a station adjacent to her building, and I told her goodnight before she stepped away.

"I already miss the Top," she said.

I smiled and said, "Same here. We'll go again."

"Alright, it's a date." She walked out onto the station plat-form and was soon swallowed by a moving matrix of pedestrians. I sat back down and the tram flew around the market district, heading down a level toward my apartment. I got off and walked without hurry through the station and into my building.

After crawling into bed and turning out the light, I lay and wondered if I'd ever get to see the Top again. I imagined it in summer—a fiery sunset and acres of lush grass waving in the cool breeze. It would be very nice, I thought. But it wasn't something I lingered on. I had to work in the morning, and I was just hoping that I'd see Sandra again, soon and very soon.

Thundersnow

X LIVED WITH A BAND OF MILITIAMEN
who held tight to a rifle from the time the sun came up until
the time it set and the whole night through. X was a young
man, but his time was never guaranteed, and neither was the
comfort of sleep or the view of a new dawn. He spent most of
his time hiding behind the brick walls of an old, barren house.
X began his days with a racing heart, and he could never fall
back asleep once it kicked in. He slept on the second floor,
where it was likely to take assassins longer to find the men,
and it would give the latter more time to ready themselves.
The first floor was set with traps and the men took a rope
ladder from a second-floor window to get in and out. X's bed
was across from the corner window, and his AR-15 sat next to
the bed through the night. They only had one mattress and a
few quilts. The men shared what they had and alternated the
mattress throughout the week. There were nine of them in
the rotation. At night, X would wake four or five times to the

drone of planes flying low across the grassland. They would survey the city and return home, and they never attacked. They would fly over again and again without a single gunshot, and X did not know why. He worried every day that the next day would be the one they decided to carpet bomb the entire area. The urban prairie was the militia's last and only line of defense outside of the city. There were militiamen in other houses there and they were much the same. They followed the same routines and hid from the same enemy.

X woke one morning that he guessed was sometime in late March. It was still cold, yet only moderately, and the snow had become a rare occurrence. He sat up and turned to grab his rifle before doing push-ups to get his blood flowing again. He held the rifle flat against the floor with both hands and completed 50 push-ups against it. He was the first to wake and once his vision cleared, he opened the window slowly and lowered the ladder. Jay had been designated night guard, and X found him walking in slow paces around the front of the house. The former's hair was in short-cut dreads wrapped underneath a knit hat. He was tall and held his rifle with tenacity, almost anxiously. "The sun's up," X said.

Jay turned to face him with sunken and tired eyes. His head hung lower than usual. "Who's takin' over?" he asked.

"I am," X said.

Jay nodded. He turned his eyes to the horizon where the sun was half-veiled with reddened clouds. "The planes flew over again last night," he said. "They circled for two hours."

He put a cigarette between his lips. "You ever feel like your heart can't slow down?"

"Maybe," X said.

"I mean…like you feel like you're never not scared?"

"Yeah," X said. "It happens a lot." Jay shook his head and looked away. The cigarette still hung there. X figured that Jay was sleep-deprived and forgot to light it.

"I can't shake it," Jay went on. "The planes—they're coming more and more, ya know? And I think there's more of 'em."

"Yeah. They keep me awake."

Jay shook his head again and sighed and sat down against the house. "I can't go inside," he said. "I can't. I really can't, X. I've been out too long."

"You don't have to," X said. "I'll be on duty 'til one." Jay nodded and put his head back and closed his eyes. X watched as the muscles in Jay's face started to relax. His cheeks lowered and his mouth, which was curled into a slight grimace, finally relaxed. His eyelids were closed but they twitched every few seconds.

"It's too much, X," he said. "I can't sleep anymore. The house is a trap. It really is."

"You can't sleep outside, though," X said. "It's too cold. You'll be hungry and freezing, and you could get hypothermia." Jay said nothing. He shifted his weight and kept his eyes closed. X crouched down next to his fellow soldier. "They'll let you have the bed if you go in," he said.

"I want to be out here," Jay said. "If something happens, I'll be ready. If I'm in there, I'm trapped. Like fish in a goddamn barrel, X. You'd be trapped, too."

"The planes won't do anything," X said. He was also reassuring himself. "You should go inside," he said again. He slung the rifle around his shoulder and stood up. "I'm going to be on guard. Don't fall asleep." At that, Jay grunted. Then he sighed. X turned away and started to pace, keeping his head on a swivel. Beyond the front of the house was an urban fringe that grew thinner and thinner until nothing was left but wasteland and dying farms. The abandoned houses that dotted the area were blocks apart, and between them, the grass had become overgrown and mercilessly choked the cracking roadways. Nature had begun taking over the area once again, and only skeletons of manmade constructs were left in its wake. A cold and unshielded breeze blew in from the open areas of the prairie. X fixed the top button of his coat and hunched his shoulders so that half of his head was beneath the collar. As the dawn passed, clouds blanketed the sky and made a formless, gray dome. X walked faster and crossed to the opposite side of the house. In the open area, a scattering of trees made it difficult to see beyond a few blocks. No one ever bothered to cut down the trees, knowing that they offered extra protection in the event of a skirmish. Between two trees, X could view another house four blocks away. He waited for the guard there to appear. After a minute, the man walked into view and glanced in X's direction. The latter raised a hand, opened it wide, and closed it into a fist. The other guard noticed and mirrored the gesture. X knew then that it was all clear at the others' house. He would return in a half-hour or so to signal the all-clear again or signal that danger was approaching. He trusted that the other guard would do the same.

After 10 minutes, X came back to the rear of the house and saw that Jay was sleeping. His back was slouched against the brick wall, and his head hung limp at his chest. Meanwhile, Q came climbing down the ladder. He was a short man with brown hair and had the rugged-rock face of a boxer. He carried a long shotgun and was the only man in the militia who could sleep at night. He greeted X and they looked down at Jay. "We should move him inside," Q said. "He's shivering."

"We'll have to wake him up," X said.

"I don't give a shit." Q bent down and pat Jay on the shoulder. When the sleeping man didn't respond, Q took his hand and gently smacked Jay's cheek. Then Jay woke up, eyes half-closed and glancing around in a daze. Q and X helped him to his feet and helped him up the ladder. As Jay lay down and immediately fell asleep again, Q tossed the quilt over him.

"Won't he suffocate?" X said. He noticed Jay's heaving breaths making the blanket rise and fall.

"That blanket's so thin, it doesn't matter," Q said. "I've slept with that thing wrapped around my head like a mummy. He'll be good." He turned to the window and went back outside. X followed him after a moment. "I'll be on duty with you for a little bit," Q said. "It's too cold not to walk and move around, ya know?" X shivered and started to pace faster, and

Q kept close by. In the open lots around the house, tall grass flowed wave-like in the wintery breeze. Abandoned houses popped up among the overgrowth and ruins of streets, as scarce as if they had been randomly tossed there. "Did House Six give the all-clear?" Q asked.

"Yeah. I checked about ten minutes ago."

"Good," Q said. "You know something? My wife used to live in that house."

"Really?"

Q nodded. "She was a teenager, I think. Her father had it built after her little brother was born and they lived about ten years there. It's a beautiful house. Or it was."

"Why'd they move out? Wasn't her father jailed?"

"Her father was the county commissioner. They put him away on revolution night." Q shook his head. "I can only hope that he's with Angie. Even if they're in a work camp, I hope they're with each other." X wasn't sure what to say in response. He wished he could tell Q that his wife and her father were re-united. But he couldn't even tell himself the location of his own family. He had used to pray every night that they were still alive, but after a year without news, he stopped. After that, he had gone another year without praying or even having a thought about God.

"When did they take her?" X asked Q.

"Just a few months after. When the work camps started up." Q sighed. "I should've been with her," he said. "It's not fair what they did."

"I don't think they've ever done anything fair."

"You know, as disgusting as they can be, it's sometimes a good thing," Q said. "It gives me all the more reason to be out here." X was about to respond with a joke about the revolution to lighten the mood when a high-pitched, familiar drone started low in the distance. He and Q instinctively stopped in their tracks. X glanced up, already knowing what it was. There was the outline of a single plane above the horizon. It was growing larger and seemed to be flying straight toward the airspace above the house. It didn't occur to X that this was the first time he had seen a plane during the day. "Stay low," Q said. The two crouched near the brush. The plane was traveling in a straight line above them, no lower and no higher than any plane would be at night. Within a minute, it was directly above. There was shouting from the direction of the other house. As X turned to look in that direction, two gunshots split the air and then there was a low bang. They were stunned by a flash of light. A thundering boom followed and like a vicious gust of wind had caught him, X was thrown backward onto the ground. He could not see anything but a blur or hear anything but ringing in his ears. All he could do was grope and try to pick up his rifle. He heard a muffled crashing sound come from behind him. Then he heard shouting. He felt a large hand grip his arm and pull upward. As his vision cleared, X saw Q pulling him onto his feet. "Let's go!" Q yelled. X picked up his rifle as Q gave him a push on the back. X didn't know where they were going, but he picked up his feet and kept close to Q and held tight to the gun. They chopped through the grass and the shouts grew louder as they ran. Rounding past a shed, Q and X found the wreckage of the plane in a large field beyond the houses and trees. There were men from another house there, and they were standing around the burning plane and holding their weapons up. One of the plane's wings was crushed between the ground and the fuselage, and the other was stuck up into the air like the fin of a great whale. The engine and nose were marred and torn apart, and the canopy was blown off. In the open cockpit was the body of the pilot, charred and mangled beyond recognition. Blackened skin dangled from pieces of bloody flesh that appeared to have been his head and rib cage. Two of the men vomited. X felt the blood rush from his face and he looked away. "What the hell happened?" Q shouted. The other men acted surprised and defenseless like little kids caught misbehaving. One man had the insignia of a first lieutenant on his field cap. He took a step toward Q and X.

"Gunners said he opened fire," the lieutenant said. "They weren't ordered to do anything. Nothing. You didn't hear his gun?" He pointed toward the pilot's body.

"No one heard shit," Q answered. "When was the last time you heard one of these planes open fire?"

"That's what I mean!" the lieutenant said, ignoring Q's insubordination. "You saying my gunners don't know aircraft ordnance when they hear it?"

"Don't get cute, Lieutenant."

"Watch your fucking step."

"It's too late to argue!" another man said. "We just revealed the position of this whole fucking militia! We're zeroed! We need to move, now!" Both Q and the lieutenant glanced around nervously. X tried to think of a plan. There were no other planes overhead and the area was silent. Amid the panicked pause, the sharp crack of a rifle rang out. One of the men dropped and held a hand up to his bleeding chest.

"Find cover!" the lieutenant shouted. The men scrambled in all directions. X ran back to the shed and ducked behind it, dropping to the ground. Jay suddenly appeared there, muttering curses as he struggled to chamber a round. X glanced in every direction and swallowed his heart, trying to sense where the shots were coming from.

"Q!" Jay yelled. "Q's down!" X heard it but didn't have a moment to think about it. He scanned the area again and again and listened. The shots seemed to be coming from every direction except the east. Men who were caught out in the open had dropped everywhere. X figured at least six casualties already. He caught glimpses of a couple of enemies out in the open but wasn't sure if they were corporation marshals or revolutionaries. X fired two shots at a man hiding behind the wreckage.

"God, forgive me," he muttered. He didn't know whether or not the bullets hit their mark. He readjusted and fired two shots at a man hunched down in the grass. Then he prayed for forgiveness again. Two men were hiding in the brush on either side of the shed, and X heard shots coming from both. He returned fire and noticed that the men began to move rapidly and low enough to be covered. X and Jay were about to be flanked.

"We need to move," Jay said. "They got us surrounded. The house should still be secure."

"Are you sure?" X asked.

"Well, anywhere has to be safer than here."

"Where is everyone?"

"I don't know, they scattered," Jay said.

X's ears were ringing but he could hear vague shouting all around. "The house is four blocks away," he said. "We can find one closer to here."

"Are any of them secure anymore?" Jay said. "Anyway, how'd we know they have ammo?" Before X could answer, a bullet tore into the siding of the shed. Chips of wood and paint sprinkled down onto X's head. He aimed and found the man trying to ambush them. X shot the gunman in the chest and asked for God's forgiveness while he reloaded. "Let's go now," Jay said. He looked at X and both men nodded. They held tight to their guns and stood up to run, heads down, in the direction of the house.

"Watch my blind side and I'll watch yours," X said. He looked around to their right as they ran, swinging the rifle back and forth as if to ward off the storm of gunfire. Beyond the shed and a couple of abandoned houses, Jay and X were in an open prairie lined with parallel roads. Their house was two blocks away. It stood tall like a brick fort among the empty grass lots. There were flurries of snow now, and they were thin, but the wind blew them into X's face. He saw a flash in his periphery and wasn't sure if it was lightning or artillery.

"Planes!" Jay yelled out.

"Goddamnit!" They both glanced upward. X saw one plane well beyond the house and another just above the open field. Its metal wings were bearing down like it was the angel of death, beastly and unstoppable. X heard the harsh drumming of the plane opening fire, and he felt his heart sink. Almost immediately, Jay took the brunt of it. Bullets shredded his chest and blood sprayed across X's side. Jay dropped to the ground and X continued to run. He ran and did not look to the sky. The plane would have to circle back to have another shot at him. He prayed that he could arrive at the house in time. The plane grew quieter for one moment as it turned. Then it grew louder again and its hellish drone was directly behind X. The latter yelled out to no one and nothing. Once again, the blaring of a machine gun resounded in the field, and X did not stop running. He jumped to the side, knowing it was a useless move. There was a sharp tug on his left shoulder and then a sting and the feeling of fire spreading. X rolled onto the grass and lay there. The droning passed by and grew silent again. Adrenaline forced X to his feet after a moment. He grabbed his rifle with his right arm and ran. Each step on the ground sent a white-hot flame through his shoulder. He could only see a blur, but muscle memory carried him back to the house. Cursing the entire time, X clambered up the ladder and crawled through the second-floor window and collapsed on the floor. His rifle slid across the room. There was no one inside. The firefight was slightly muted now. As minutes passed, it grew quieter and the shots grew less frequent. There were low rumbles of thunder in the air. Snow flurries made it through the open window and landed on X's face, the mild sting helping him stay conscious. He took his coat and shirt off and tried for 10 minutes to create a bandage. He found some of the men's spare shirts and tucked them against the entrance and exit wounds and wrapped another shirt around the entire shoulder. Before knotting it, he shoved an additional shirt into his mouth and screamed into it as he struggled to position his hands properly. The wrapping shirt slipped out of his hand once, twice, and three times. His eyes burned and he couldn't see anything, so X trusted the feeling in his hands. He got the knot started, but then it fell apart once, twice, three times, and four times before it stuck, and X used his teeth to pull it tight. As the knot pressed the shirts against his wound, his vision faded into a tornado of color. He lost consciousness and slipped down, falling flat on the floor.

There were still flurries when X woke up, and he could no longer hear gunfire nearby or anywhere. There was a faint smell of smoke. X crawled silently to the bedroom window and glanced out toward the urban fringe. There were three helicopters scattered around on empty townhouse roofs. Their rotors were still spinning, and on each door was painted a maroon "V" in large lettering. X glanced at them for only a second before slipping back onto the floor. He had no sinking feeling of dread. He felt only indifference, as if he had already known the choppers would be there. The corporation marshals were taking over, but X knew the truth—they had been in control for months. He breathed deeply and lay down, staring at the ceiling. There was a small fan there that was surrounded by glow-in-the-dark stars and crescent moons tacked to the ceiling. They were the same kind of stars that X had above his bed when he was a boy. The house whistled in the cold wind, but it was the only sound. X didn't know if the marshals were sweeping the area or not. If they were, he wouldn't have heard them anyway. Maybe the militia would find him first and rescue him, he thought. Or maybe the marshals would find him. Maybe they wouldn't. And maybe, in another life, he would have a family and a home, and the planes overhead would only be travelers flying to brighter parts of the land.

The Punch-Drunk Sky

IT WAS MARCH OF 1920, nearly two years after the war that split our country apart and transformed it into a bloody and divided aristocracy. I was seated behind the wheel of a bomber and surrounded by the drone of its twin engines chopping through a cold and clear night. Known to us as "The Beast," the giant of a plane glided 700 feet from the ground where wasteland and struggling farms rested under the stars. I watched the moon as it gave the world a pale glow and poured starry light through my window. It was all so quiet and I breathed easy. But in the back of my mind, I remembered why I was piloting The Beast and what could've been waiting ahead in the darkness. He wasn't in my sights, but I knew the guard was somewhere in the skyway and flying ahead to keep watch. His plane was faster and more agile, and he was a better pilot than I was. Even now, I still say that he was the best pilot I've ever seen. Yet somehow, he was also the worst. His name was Madox Hampton, and he flew differently from every other pilot

I had ever known. He flew as if he didn't care and as if gravity had no effect on him. He maneuvered in ways that no one else would dare to try, and it didn't always work out well, but he did it anyway and he made up ways to survive. He didn't only survive, however. Madox was an ace. He was a dead-eye and a terror of the skies.

Our nightly missions always required a guard, and any mission required a guard when The Beast was involved. So, Madox led the way as we traveled. The alarm clock I had mounted to the dashboard read 0102. Eddie Nemeth sat in the turret at the nose of The Beast, hunched over and asleep. Behind me, half of The Beast's fuselage served as a passengers' cabin, and the other half was a thick metal tube filled with 32 bombs. There were four switches on the right side of my steering wheel and they each released a barrage of eight bombs. Our drop location was on a map that I stuck to the front window using a piece of chewing gum. The location wouldn't be lit, our commander told me. I would have to gauge where to drop the bombs by looking for the moon's reflection on rivers and where the tree lines began and ended.

The location was only minutes away now. I descended to 500 feet and leveled out for a minute before dipping lower, but at a slower rate. The altimeter crept up toward zero, but it was moving slow enough to go unnoticed. 400 feet now. I kept my eyes on the ground. There was a river ahead, and I could see a shimmery white light on it that stretched perpendicular to my flight path. Past the river would be a few stretches of wooded

land and scorched pastures. The map showed that the target
was in a hollow just before a second river. I estimated it was
about two minutes away, and then I stopped to glance at the
altimeter. 300 feet. Before I looked up, there was a sound like
a muted boom. While I searched for the source, I saw a distant
flash of light. It was a bright speck in the dark space ahead, and
my heart began to race. I didn't even have a moment to be fear-
ful and think the worst. "Nemeth!" I yelled. There was a rum-
bling of distant gunfire. I banged on the front window of the
cabin. "Nemeth! Get up! Get up, dammit!" Nemeth stirred and
a few seconds passed before he put his head up. "Shots fired!"
I screamed over the roar of the engines. "Somethin' was hit!"
Nemeth nodded to me this time and positioned himself behind
the gun. The sound of gunfire and other engines grew louder.
Tracers soared at random through the sky like miniature com-
ets. They grew brighter and I was ready to make a big turn.
The Beast was not fast and she couldn't turn on a dime, but I
was prepared to crank the wheel as far as it could go. Nemeth
turned to yell something to me, and I couldn't make out every
word. It sounded like "I can't see." Suddenly, a fighter plane
appeared at point-blank like a winged demon. It came from
the darkness and passed above us. Nemeth aimed the turret up
to take a few potshots. The plane was dark and striped on the
wings. It wasn't Madox or any of our other pilots. It was House
Coralis. I glanced back and watched as the fighter turned to his
right and the moonlight gleamed off his engine block. Then I
remembered that we didn't have a rear gunner. The tail of The

Beast was fully exposed. Tightening my grip on the wheel, I turned sharply to the left and pushed the throttle. The Beast dipped for a moment, then lurched upward. The engines' growl became deeper as they strained to pull the plane higher. I knew that The Beast was not fast enough to turn and meet the Coralis pilot head-on, but I knew if I could yaw left, that would give Nemeth a better shooting angle. The Beast groaned as I kept her turning. I glanced out the window and saw the enemy flying straight toward the nose where the turret was situated. Nemeth was steadying himself and began to fire. I wasn't sure what was causing it, maybe it was the awkward angle of the moonlight and the shadows it cast, but Nemeth couldn't hit anything. He held the trigger for a full five seconds with no results. I started to see the Coralis' tracers fly past me. A couple of them left blackened burn marks as they streaked past the front window. I realized that that moment might've been my last. As the noise of the plane engines and the rip of bullets grew louder, I closed my eyes. My hands tightened around the wheel. We were still turning. I heard glass shatter and I winced. The moment that followed, I thought I was dead. I didn't know if I blacked out or not. There was a hailstorm of bullets outside the window and then a bright flash. I opened my eyes and waited for the colors and dark spots to disappear. When I could see outside, I noticed there were no longer any tracers in the sky. For a moment, there was only darkness. I glanced downward. Beneath The Beast and off to the left was a smaller fighter, lighter in color and rolling smoothly from side to side. In its cockpit, under the faint glow of the moon, I could see an orange winter cap, its tail fluttering in the wind. Beyond the fighter was the Coralis plane. It was spewing flames and tipping forward before it fell into a straight and downward spiral. I was straining to see, but I believed that I saw a hand extend from that orange-capped pilot and that it waved at me. "Madox!" I said, laughing. Regardless of where he had come from and what he did to shoot the Coralis down, he was there. We were facing a squadron of other Coralis planes now, but I could still see Madox in my periphery as he flew next to me. I hadn't yet noticed that Nemeth was lying crumpled up in the turret, riddled with bullets from head to toe. Blood was seeping from the turret and into the cabin, where it pooled up against the edge of my boot. There was no defense between the Coralis and me, except for Madox's single-gunned fighter. Four planes appeared and were flying toward us. My hands tightened around the wheel. I couldn't see Madox anymore. His plane had raced forward and he started to distance himself from me. Within a few seconds, he was hundreds of yards ahead, and tracers began to fill the night sky again. I started to descend and hoped that Madox's engagement would draw the Coralis fighters upward and away from The Beast. Flying slow and making a gradual descent, I watched. Madox dipped down and immediately pulled upward when the Coralis reached him. He flew directly vertical for a few seconds and neared a stall as he fired at the underbelly of the first plane. Then Madox leveled out and went into an Immelmann turn, keeping a bead on the first plane's tail. He fired a few bursts and trailed the plane.

Just as the other Coralis pilots moved into firing range, Madox fired two more bursts. I watched his tracers as they connected with the first plane. It immediately turned into a barrel roll and started to spin in small circles and fall toward Earth. Madox pulled up without hesitation and went vertical. The second Coralis flew underneath him. Madox approached a stall, and his plane seemed to stop before pitching downward and to the left. He leveled out and then turned toward the Coralis in an instant, as if his plane had pivoted midair on the head of a pin. He had just neared a stall only a second before. It was an unnatural movement. I blinked and couldn't believe what I had seen. I was still descending when Madox's bullets connected with the fighter. Its engine began to spit flames, and Madox was already turning around. He made a single helix and positioned himself behind the two pilots that were left. He had flown so near to them during the fight that their bullets put tears in his canvas. The torn pieces of fabric looked like streamers flapping against Madox's fuselage. The tears were just next to the cockpit and inches away from where he sat.

Now, what happened in the minutes following couldn't be believed even if it were fiction. I was flying The Beast by instinct only, and my eyes were skyward as I watched Madox remove every threat of death that flew around me. The three planes chased each other above me, and Madox was flying just a few feet behind one of the Coralis, firing bursts into the plane's fuselage. He was so close to the Coralis fighter that the wingman couldn't take a shot without it being friendly fire.

Within seconds, Madox had taken the first one of them down. The fighter that was trailing him was safe and ready to shoot. But as the second pilot fired his initial burst, Madox veered upward and to the right. He corkscrewed and started downward again. The Coralis followed the maneuver and continued tight on Madox's tail. He fired but failed to connect, and then Madox barrel-rolled before dipping downward. His plane started to level out and the Coralis made a sharp left turn, trying to reverse and catch Madox as he recovered from the move. But the latter was ready. He turned upward and performed an Immelmann at 45 degrees. When the Coralis was turned around, Madox was ready and tracers began to fly. They punctured the front of the fighter, and Madox held down the trigger until he was a second away from colliding with the other plane. Once he pulled up, the Coralis' engine was in flames, and its propeller was spinning slowly and splintered into pieces. I released a breath that I didn't realize I was holding. The sky was now empty darkness and free of the spark of tracers and the sound of gunfire. The Coralis fighter was arcing downward like a falling star. Madox flew a wide circle and made his way toward me, passing me in the opposite direction. I saw a flash of his face in the moonlight. The tail of his hat waved in the wind behind him, and his plane was flying smoothly and slowly. He gave me an all-clear hand wave, and before he turned to follow in my flight path, I saw a small gleam of white below his hat. Shreds of his plane were torn from the fuselage and he was sitting at the helm of the thing with a smile on his face.

I circled back, and after looking at the map, I found the drop location. We had passed it by about one mile. I pulled down on both levers, and soon the night sky was lit with a fiery brilliance from the destruction below. I watched the explosions, still laughing to myself in disbelief. Madox faced five Coralis planes without assistance and he emerged with five victories.

We made the return flight with ease and landed in the air-field just after 0140. The strip was flanked by two rows of lanterns, which were quickly extinguished after our planes touched down. Major Jarvis and two corporals came out to meet us. The Major stared in disbelief at Madox's tattered plane. "What happened?" he asked. I stepped down from the cabin of The Beast. Madox walked up behind me, unbuttoning his jacket.

"Coralis, sir," I said. "We lost Nemeth."

The Major shook his head and asked, "How did they know we were there?"

"I don't know," I said.

"They must have an airfield nearby," Madox said. "No one saw them coming."

"How many?" the Major asked.

"Five," Madox said.

"Christ," he sighed. "Did you make it to the target?" I told him we did and that the bombing went as planned. "Good," the Major said. "We'll need more observation. An ambush like this can't happen again." He looked at Madox's plane and shook his head. Then he looked at its pilot. "How did you make it out alive?" he asked.

"I shot them before they shot me," Madox said.

The Major scoffed. "Not before they tore your plane to shreds," he said. "We'll have to hand it over to the mechanics again."

"I can cover the cost this time," Madox said. He broadened his shoulders and breathed in deeply. "It's my plane; thus, it's my responsibility."

"Do as you wish," Major Jarvis said. He reached into his pocket and produced two envelopes. "While we're on the topic, here are this week's advances," he said. "Expect a briefing sometime soon. There's going to be a new offensive by the end of the month."

"What type of offensive?" I asked.

"A big one," the Major said. He instructed the two corporals to bring the planes into the hangar before turning to walk away.

"Sir, we need to take care of Nemeth's body," I said. "He's still in The Beast."

The Major glanced at the turret of the bomber. Then he turned to me and said, "Bring him behind the hangar. I'll look at hiring a new gunner right away."

Both of the corporals helped as Madox and I carried Nemeth from the plane and put him in a body bag. We moved slowly to avoid spilling the gore of his chest. The corporals laid him down behind the hangar and began preparations to bring the body to Nemeth's family in the city. Madox and I went to the barracks. There were railroad ties stacked outside there and we sat down on them. He offered me a cigarette and I accepted. I didn't feel like sleeping yet. "What do you know about this new offensive?" I asked.

"Not much," Madox said. "I don't think that the officers do either. It sounds as if they're making new plans every day."

"I don't know about it," I said. "A great big attack after we took a beating at Forest Field? Coralis is going to come at us in droves. I don't know if it's a smart idea."

"It will be fun, though," Madox said.

"Fun?"

"I'm looking forward to a challenge," Madox continued. "House Coralis has some of the best pilots in the world, you know. Won't it be great to say that we took a dozen of them down? That we fought hard and won?"

"I'll be happy if the offensive succeeds," I said.

"Well, if there are no Coralis fighters left, then it'll certainly succeed alright," Madox said. "I'll do my damnedest to make sure of that."

"You're definitely the best at it," I said.

"Oh, please. You're making me blush," Madox said. He put a hand up to his face as if to hide it. We laughed and then smoked in silence. Madox was looking upward, apparently thinking.

"You know, I was thinking that you could use a second gun," I said. "Or maybe some armor for your plane. After what happened tonight, your luck is due to run out soon."

Madox shook his head. "No such thing as luck, friend. A gun is only as good as the pilot who uses it. I get along just fine with one."

"Well, I'm sure another couldn't hurt," I said. "Are you telling me you claimed all your victories just by flying well?" Madox didn't respond. He twiddled with the envelope and looked into the distance. "We've been in the service of this house for almost two years," I said. "You get closer to death with every mission. If those Coralis were better shots, the bullets they put in your plane earlier would've been in your gut."

"But they weren't," Madox said. He looked at me sternly. "I'll be fine," he said. "If it were easy, then none of us would ever have become a skilled pilot. It has to be dangerous some of the time. Hell, it does most of the time."

"You truly don't care, do you?"

"About what?"

"Death."

"Well," Madox said, "not when I'm in the air." I looked at him skeptically. He continued, "There's only one thing that matters to me then."

"And what's that?" I asked.

"Flying," Madox said. He shrugged. "When you're in the air, what else is there?"

"I'm serious," I said. "You're going to get yourself killed."

"I'm serious too."

"What about?"

"About not caring."

"You don't care if you die?"

Madox shrugged. He said, "No. Not particularly."

I couldn't believe it. My friend was going to get himself killed, and he didn't give a damn. "Well, then, everything makes sense," I said. "You're just dense. There's nothing else to say about it. You're just reckless and stupid." Madox took a deep breath and was about to speak; thought better of it. He went silent and I watched him, waiting. "You don't have anything to say about that?" I said. "Do you think I want to see you get taken down? Burning alive in your cockpit while I'm forced to watch? It could happen at any point. For Christ's sake, you were inches away from a having bullet in your chest tonight. Doesn't that scare you, even just a bit?"

"Maybe you're right," Madox said. He refused to look at me. He just stared straight ahead and took a drag from the cigarette. "But you know what?" he said. "You're sitting next to me right now, are you not?" Now, he turned around to look at me and poked a finger into my chest as he spoke. "Did you even think about that?" he said. "Do you think I want to see you get taken down? Sitting there in your bomber, body full of bullets? Hell, look at Nemeth. And he's far from being the first. I didn't—I don't—want that to be you. Did you think about that?" I didn't respond, knowing Madox was right. I just hated the thought of him dead with no one to blame but himself. I knew I couldn't say anything to make him stop flying with reckless abandon, but I did it anyway, perhaps because it made me feel just a little bit better. Meanwhile, Madox stood up and paced around, again refusing to look at me as he smoked the cigarette down to the end. He rambled on. "Did the war numb all of us this terribly? There are so many bodies now that we treat 'em like dust in a garbage bin. There's a new one every week. We're a commodity for all House Scioto cares, and we're completely complacent. Why? Because we get paid and paid handsomely. But what's all that money really worth? Nothing. Get in, get out, try not to die, and if you survive, here's your pay." He sat back down and sighed. "You know, at least during the war we had something worth fighting for."

A few moments later, the front door of the barracks opened and Ben Edelman, an English expatriate gunner, came out to join us. He was dressed in an undershirt and shorts. I offered him a smoke as he explained that he couldn't sleep. "I caught wind of the offensive," he said. "Can't exactly rest when you know you're gonna be taking on half the Coralis in a week." He added that his contract was set to expire at the end of March, but I already knew it because mine was as well. Edelman went on and told us how he wanted to take his earnings and buy a farm in the old heartland. There were flat fields and peace there. "I'd like a quiet place," he said. "Either north or west of here. Somewhere I could get lost in the fields." He paused. "There's still farmland in the North, you know—miles of it. I heard that it's all public property."

"You mean there are squatter's rights there?" Madox said.

"Something like that, I'm sure. Whatever it is, I plan to build myself a nice farmhouse and look out every morning on about two hundred acres of corn." At that, Madox scoffed. "Pardon?" Edelman said.

"Farmland and no one around for miles. I'd go crazy," Madox said.

"Well, what's your idea of paradise?" Edelman asked.

Madox sat back and crossed his arms. "I'd like a southern town," he said. "Lots of girls. And friendly people enjoying the sunshine."

"House St. Croix owns most of the South," I said. "The coast is locked up tight."

Madox continued like he didn't hear anything. "I had a sister down there," he said. "She managed a YWCA, last I heard from her. That was…well, that was four years ago. Haven't heard from her since then. But you know, St. Croix is a free land. No landholdings and no aristocracy. What more could you want?"

I wondered for a moment where Madox was from. He had never told me. "You believe she's still there?" I asked.

"Of course she is," Madox said. "She's my sister, after all. Hamptons aren't the milksop type. If she had to, she'd probably be on the roof of that YWCA building with a shotgun." He went on to describe the hypothetical scene: his sister sitting on a rocking chair with a shotgun on her lap and letting shells fly at whoever dared tell her to give up her property. That made Edelman laugh. He took a final drag of his cigarette and flicked it toward the dirt road.

"It's been a long night, gentlemen," he said. "Now it's time to get some sleep."

"I'm sure the Major is going to wake us up for a meeting at 0600," Madox said.

I sighed and said, "Doesn't he always?"

Madox didn't speak to me again that night. We went back into the barracks and tried to sleep. For a couple of hours, I was able to rest and dream about the end of my contract, only weeks away in reality. I had left the airfield and went to find my family. They were alive and on a thriving farm somewhere in the quiet Midwest. It was a lovely dream and I didn't let go of it, even after I woke up and birds were outside the window and chirping loud in the music of spring.

There were two briefings before the offensive. The second was the afternoon before the attack, and it outlined the final plan we would be executing. Major Jarvis summarized it by saying, "Bomb each and every one of the locations, and shoot down as much Coralis aircraft as possible." A majority of our group would be flying—18 planes. I was instructed to fly one of our single-engine bombers which carried a load of 18 bombs. Unlike The Beast, it had an open cockpit and there was a gunner's turret behind the pilot's seat. Edelman had never completed his flight training, so he was assigned to be my gunner. Madox would serve as my wingman and guard. There would only be two bombers, each assigned to three drop locations, all of which were armories and warehouses. Major Jarvis told the group that he anticipated a long fight but once we'd have the advantage in. "Once they see us in the sky, there will be an airfield of about twenty units that should deploy," he said. "Until then, fly high enough to avoid the anti-aircraft guns and there should be no problem. We'll hit them before they know what's happening." He pointed to the map of House Coralis. "This is the 'land beyond the river,'" he said. "It belongs to House Scioto and we're going to take it back, one piece at a time. It should be easy for the militia to move in once we're done with 'em today. I know that many of your contracts will be expiring at the end of the month. For you, this will be your last offensive. Let's make it count, men." Then we left the tent in silence, and I could still hear the Major's words in my head as we walked toward the airfield. Corporal Young approached me and asked if I wanted to place a bet. He held a notepad and pencil in his hand.

"How many victories do you think Hampton'll get today?" he said. "We've got some high bets here. What'd you say?" I asked him what the others bet. Young looked at the notepad. "Trevino says four," he said. "I say five, and that's the highest bet so far."

Madox appeared at my side. "I bet twenty," he said.

"Jesus Lord," Young said, "that's not even possible." He shook his head, then he looked up and saw it was Madox. "Wait a minute. You can't bet," he said. He laughed and then Madox started to laugh. I smiled and handed Young a few dollars. I told him I bet six planes and that if Madox could do it, then I'd give all the winnings straight to him.

Madox clapped a hand on my shoulder and said, "Friend, if I can get six victories today, I'll give you my entire pay for the month."

"You wouldn't dare," I said. Madox extended his hand. I looked at it for a second, confused.

"I'm serious," he said. "Shake my hand." I did so. "One month's pay, coming right up," he said, pulling his goggles over his eyes. He climbed into his plane and gave us a salute. Then Young looked at me and shook his head. We turned away and boarded our planes. Edelman climbed into the turret behind me and handed me a spare drum magazine.

"You never know," he said. "It could come in handy. One of mine jammed once and I dropped it when I tried to fix it. Almost all the rounds were still inside. Completely wasted." I thanked him and placed it next to the rest of my ammunition. There was a single machine gun on top of the engine block for me to use. After sitting down, I unfolded a map that showed all of the drop locations marked with bright red ink, and I pinned it to the left-hand side of the cockpit with thumbtacks and mounted a compass off to its side. Elsewhere, someone yelled "contact!" and the sputtering of an engine echoed across the airfield before it turned into a low hum. As I buckled myself in, I heard two more planes start around us. Then I flipped the bomber's ignition switch as the mechanic thrust down on the propeller. In seconds, the entire airfield was abuzz. We rolled down the patchy strip of grass in unison and eventually felt the ground disappear from under us. Madox was ahead of me, rolling left and right and back again, as if he was just going for a leisurely fly.

When we reached the western border of House Scioto, there was nothing ahead but an evening sky full of bright, orange light and pastel clouds. I looked down at the map and turned slightly left. Madox, flying next to us, nodded and followed. I prayed that I would be able to get at least one barrage done before Coralis found us. And as if to mock me, a shell exploded several yards away. I turned away from it. "Hell! We just got here!" Edelman yelled. I looked at the map again. The drop location was close. Madox had already split with us to distract and take out the artillery. I was counting down the seconds until we'd see Coralis planes swarming down on us like predators. Edelman sat with his hand on the trigger for when they did. We were just high enough now to avoid more artillery. After a moment, I saw the Coralis armory below us and pulled the switch. Six bombs went sailing downward, and we heard the boom of ground-shaking explosions. "Two to go!" Edelman said. A second later, he tapped me on the shoulder and pointed upward. It was hard to see as the setting sun was in my eyes, but there looked to be about 10 or so Coralis fighters bearing down on us from the southwest sky.

I shook my head. "Son of a bitch." Edelman aimed his gun and began to fire. Rarely did I fly the bomber we were in, so I wasn't used to the sound of a machine gun directly behind my head, and it was deafening and distracting. I kept my eyes on the map and made a beeline for the second target. Above, Madox had returned and was rushing upward to engage the Coralis at the side of some of our other pilots. They split the Coralis ranks down the middle, and the enemy planes rearranged themselves to meet the threat. I stayed just low enough to avoid the fight and just high enough to keep the Coralis artillery away.

"He's got one!" Edelman called out. He laughed, "That's one for Hampton already." I told him to shut up and focus. But a minute later, he loudly announced Madox's second victory. I said nothing. The next location was just ahead.

"Keep any stray off our backs," I yelled out. Edelman turned the gun around and protected our rear. I pitched the bomber downward and closer to the target before pulling the switch. The second slew of bombs was away. I waited to hear the drumming of Edelman's gun, but there was nothing. I glanced back for just a moment. There were about three Coralis planes near our tail, and Madox was giving them a hard time. They couldn't break from their pattern without Madox taking shots at them or blocking their flight path with a close and sudden maneuver. In the seconds that I had glanced backward, Madox took one of them out. Edelman watched, relaxing his hands on the gun and staring in disbelief. There were more Coralis planes now, but Madox was taking them out at an easy pace. They swarmed him three at a time, but he was too quick and too precise to make an easy target for them. "God," I said. "There're a hundred of the bastards."

Edelman shook his head. "We should've been dead by now." I wanted to continue watching the spectacle that was Madox Hampton, but the third location was farther away, so I had to constantly check the map. As I glanced up, I noticed a Coralis fighter at our three o'clock. I yelled out to Edelman, but it was too late. I heard gunfire and the whizz of rounds flying through our fuselage. There was a rush of wind as I ducked. The plane cast a shadow on us as it flew over, and I caught just a glimpse of the Coralis' landing gear above my head. Edelman cursed and turned his gun to the opposite side. The plane was turning around to make another pass. Before the pilot had found his shooting angle, Edelman put a couple of bullets through his wing, sending him down and out of range. I watched the plane dip below us and begin to helix upward, preparing to come down on us from above. I pitched the bomber downward to give Edelman a legitimate shooting angle, but the Coralis fighter was much faster and was already arcing downward, ready to fire. "Get us lower! Lower!" Edelman yelled.

I pitched downward and muttered, "C'mon Madox, where are you?" Then the Coralis plane opened fire. I yelled at Edelman to hold on and pitched upward to face the gunfire head-on. Edelman swung around and began shooting above my head at the plane. We were seconds away from colliding. I rolled to the right and veered off the flight path, going downward again. The Coralis fighter followed. Now, he was at our six. Before Edelman could get a shot off, the Coralis dipped down and out of range. Edelman would've had to shoot through our fuselage to hit him.

"Down!" he yelled out. But we were out of time. I pitched downward and there was already gunfire. I felt bullets strike the underside of the bomber, rattling the wood panels under my feet. I yawed left and tried to pull away. I heard Edelman yell out in pain. And the gunfire still drummed on. Just as I pitched right, attempting a zig-zag pattern, I saw another plane at our

12 o'clock. Silhouetted against the coral sky, it came right toward us at a startling speed. My hand was on the trigger. But I
waited. The pilot extended an arm and motioned to me to pitch
down. I didn't hesitate. We dove downward and I lost sight for
a moment. The mystery plane rushed over us, its gun blasting
without rest. I couldn't turn to watch but heard a couple of low
bangs. The gunfire continued for a moment, then it seemed to
stop all at once. I leveled out the bomber and glanced back to
see what had happened. "Oh no," Edelman moaned. "No, no,
no!" He was laying back in the turret, holding a bloody hand
against his thigh. I thought he was moaning about the bullet
in his leg, but when I glanced up, I found the true reason. My
suspicions were confirmed—the angel who came to our rescue
was Madox. But his plane was missing its propeller. As I turned
the bomber around, I saw his engine begin to spit flames. And
now he was descending toward Earth, more silent and still than
I had ever seen him before. I wanted to follow him down, even
in death, letting the breeze carry us to the ground. But one location still needed to be hit, and there was a squadron of Coralis planes not far behind. The least I could do for Madox was
let the mission succeed. I bit my tongue to fight back the tears
and told Edelman to hold on. Then I turned the bomber west
toward our last target. It was a tall, unguarded warehouse, and
I dropped the last few shells on it as soon as we arrived, setting
the evening air alight with fire. I flipped the switch back to close
the bomb bay doors and turned the plane back east and toward
home. The sky was nearly empty now. A small formation of

Coralis fighters was in the distance, flying low and in a loose pattern that suggested a retreat. I could see a few Scioto pilots scattered throughout the sky. "Get him," Edelman said.

"What?"

"Get Hampton. We can't leave him there. Dead or alive, he's your friend."

"But your leg," I said.

"I'll make it just fine," Edelman said. "Just go." I didn't wait and pushed the throttle forward. We raced ahead, free of the weight of the bombs. It was easy to find where Madox went down. A column of thin, black smoke reached toward the heavens from a low and muddy valley. I could see that Madox's entire plane was in flames and already burned down to its skeletal frame. I found a level strip of land nearby and descended into it. As we touched ground, the propeller chopped bits of prairie grass and tall brush and spat them back into the cockpit. I covered my face with one arm until the bomber came to a stop and everything was silent. I looked up and promised Edelman that I would be quick. He answered with a groan that sounded vaguely like "okay." Then I jumped out of the bomber, running through the field and flinging my arms outward to push back the brush. The wreckage was just a minute away. The flames had died a bit, but it still burned hot, and I felt the heat on my face. Blackened sections of the frame were starting to deteriorate and collapse. I couldn't make out anything in the cockpit that resembled a body, only a charred seat and set of controls.

"Oh God, tell me that he didn't jump," I said. Fearing the sight of a body, I sprinted around the wreckage and looked for Madox. There was nothing in the field but some stray sections of the plane and long, muddy grooves where Madox had started to land. Wait now…why are these ruts so long? I thought. I glanced up at the plane again and realized that the thing was completely intact, barring the fire it had endured. The engine wasn't dented and the frame hadn't been crumpled by impact. Before I could make a decision or even come to a conclusion, I heard a sharp whistle. It was coming from somewhere near where I had landed. A second later, there was another whistle. I started toward the bomber, running faster this time. When I cleared the brush and found the plane again, it was a beautiful and relieving sight. There he was, the immortal bastard, kneeling on top of the fuselage and making a tourniquet for Edelman.

"We can't waste any time, friend," he said, not skipping a beat. "He needs to get to a medic as soon as possible."

"You're right," I said. But I stood frozen, wiping a tear from my eye. Madox finished the tourniquet and jumped down and put a hand on my shoulder.

"You didn't think I'd let that Coralis shoot you from behind, did you?" he said.

"You've…you've outdone yourself," I said. "I don't even know what to say."

"Well, you were right after all," he said. "I'm quite stupid." He gestured toward the smoking wreckage across the field. "Just look at what I put her through." I laughed, relieved.

"Now, let's fly," Madox said. I didn't hesitate and jumped into the cockpit. He thrust down on the propeller and I started the engine. Then Madox planted his feet on the bottom wing and anchored one arm around the lip of the cockpit and the other on Edelman, who was silently suffering in the turret behind me. We flew fast and true on the way back to the airfield. Madox had his eyes forward the entire time, wearing a strange, wry smile on his face. His orange cap whipped in the wind behind him like a proud victory flag. Even when he lost, he still won.

Sleep came easy the night after the offensive, and I woke in the morning to the news that Edelman was doing well. He couldn't put any weight on his leg, but it wasn't infected, and the medic told me that he was already cracking jokes about becoming "lame." But the medic refuted it, saying, "I don't foresee that happening." I thanked him for taking care of Edelman, then I left for the barracks. The other pilots were there, sitting around a table and shooting dice and telling stories. Madox admitted to us that he only had five victories during the fight, to which we still gave huge applause. Meanwhile, Young collected his money from everyone, laughed, and thanked us all—especially Madox—for the added income.

In the afternoon, Madox left for the hangar to see the new plane he bought for himself. Then evening came, and I was sufficiently bored without the adrenaline of being up in the air. A few of us still in the barracks decided to go into town for a few hours and loosen up. Young was going to drive us there in his car. I went out to ask Madox if he wanted to join. "Thanks, but I'm going to stay here and touch up the new bird," he said, slapping a greasy rag onto his shoulder. Other than one old mechanic, he was the only person in the hangar. He had draped his coat over the wing of his new plane, an old but fast S.E.5. It was a light silver color and small and sleek. It was rare to see Madox near a plane without him being in the cockpit. I said that he should join us and that there would be whiskey and beautiful women in the city. "A tempting offer," he said. He winked and added, "But I'll be a good man and let you have them all to yourself." I told him he was crazy. "I already knew that, friend," he said.

That made me smile. I paused and was about to leave, but stopped. "You know," I said, "I should thank you for saving me. And Edelman, for that matter."

"That's not necessary," Madox said. "You're here. That's what's important."

"I know that."

"You can repay me by sticking around a while longer," Madox continued. He smiled. "Your friendship will do." I offered the night out once more, and Madox declined once more. We shook hands, and as I left, I stopped once to look back. He was already intent on his engine, tinkering away at the rotor. So, I turned around and left for the barracks to wash up. As I put on my cleanest blue shirt, Young stopped by my room.

"The train departs at 2000," he said, "so don't miss it. I've got a pocket full of bills now, and there are three pints of beer calling my name."

"I'll be there," I said. "I just need to pick up my money first." Young gave the OK hand sign and bounded away excitedly, as if he were already drunk. I put on a dark jacket and hat and walked to the other side of the compound where Major Jarvis' office sat. He was inside, standing over his desk and organizing a stack of paper bills and documents. "Major," I said.

"Yes, Sharpe. You're here for your compensation?"

"Yes, sir," I said. The Major picked up a stack of dollar bills and began counting. He said that he was just finishing up payroll duties for the week.

"I also need to ask a favor of you," he said. "Could you give Hampton his discharge papers? He hasn't come in to get them yet."

"Discharge papers?" I asked.

"I figured he'd want to take them before he leaves," the Major said. He must've seen the confusion in my face, because he continued, "His contract was up six weeks ago. He didn't come in to renew it when some of the others did back in December." The Major cut the stack of dollar bills and handed half of it to me. "I told him he'd be discharged well before the offensive, but he insisted on staying."

"Why?"

"He told me that you needed a guard," the Major said. "One who was experienced, at least." He added that Madox hadn't stopped to pick up his compensation either. Scioto accountants divided it among everyone who had flown the offensive. Hardly able to think anymore, I thanked the Major and took my money, then returned to the barracks where it was empty and quiet. I passed by Madox's room and he wasn't there. It was completely bare apart from the bed and nightstand, but Madox never had any personal belongings there anyway. There was no one else around, so I returned to my room and found a note next to my bed. I unfolded it and sat down to read it.

Sharpe, I suppose this was the best goodbye I could come up with. Forgive me, I'm not good at saying farewell.

The mechanics were able to install an additional fuel line, so my trip should be quick and easy. Regardless, I'll look for stops along the way with some good St. Croix folks. They treated my family well for years.

Don't be afraid to be bold. I've seen you in the air, and I know you're capable of doing anything you want to. If you are feeling brazen, then perhaps one day you can take your pay and fly down here to visit. Then we can reunite and fly together again, somewhere without bullets and bombs, and we can breathe in the fresh air. I look forward to the day.

Until later, friend.

I glanced through the window and saw an open door at the end of the hangar. A mechanic passed by and pulled the door closed. I opened the window and looked up to the sky and listened for an engine. There was nothing. Outside, the sun was setting and made the clouds a deep orange. I walked out to the airfield and offered a cigarette to the mechanic. He was leaving the hangar as I passed by. "Do you know when he left?" I asked.

"Ah, it was about a half-hour ago," he said. "I just been working around the place, so I opened the door for 'im. He filled his tank all the way up to the top and that was all. No luggage or anything. Snatched my apple on the way out." He shrugged. "I was gonna eat it later, but oh well."

"Did he say anything to you?"

"Nothing," the mechanic said. "Just had a big grin on his face when he pulled outta the hangar. He went out right away—just took off." I smiled and looked up toward the sky. The air was still and the clouds had not moved. They only changed color, transforming into a brilliant kaleidoscope along the horizon. Madox had just flown south with nothing but the clothes on his back. And I knew he was probably laughing to himself, thinking about the wild and deadly skies he once commanded.

Lost City Road

THE COFFEE DRIPPED SLOWLY and was close to filling the pot. Orion liked the way it dripped because he thought it was consistent and aesthetically pleasing. The smell that filled the house was also pleasant. He got into the habit of making a pot every morning before work, giving himself enough time to relax and drink it slowly. He had been doing it for years, even before the civil war had laid waste to the city. It was easy for him and the ritual was comforting. His mother loved it just as much. In the winter, the house was drafty, and hot coffee was the easiest way to get warm.

As his mother Gloria lay in her room, Orion waited for the last drop to fall. Then he grabbed the pot and squinched two mugs in one hand. He walked into the bedroom. "Thank God you're up," Gloria said. She rubbed her eyes and sat up. "I might've frozen to death in here." Orion set the mugs on the nightstand and poured coffee into both. Gloria picked one of them up, cupped it with both hands, and yawned. She brought it to her lips, stopped, then looked over at Orion. "You take it black now?"

"Oh yeah," he said. He sat down next to the bed. "I've been drinking it black for a while now. You didn't notice?" Gloria shook her head. "I just figured that it's more manly," Orion said.

"Is that right?"

"Yeah."

She rolled her eyes and sipped the coffee. "Well, I don't see you as some kinda 'alpha,'" she said. "You're still my little boy."

"Ma, I'm old enough to drink…legally." They both laughed at the word "legally." Orion took a sip of the coffee and looked around. "Are the kids at school?"

"They aren't going today."

"What? Why not?" he asked. The snow they had wasn't more than an inch.

"Gang stuff," she said. Her eyes fell. "There's been some things going on…shootings east of here. Right on the kids' route."

"Shootings? Where'd you hear this from?"

"Tracy."

"Ah, she just likes to gossip," Orion said. He paused. "She say what gang it was?"

"I dunno, but apparently they're getting violent. Hell, they all are."

"So, when will the kids go back?"

"I'll let 'em wait," Gloria said. "Things always clear up after a while. That's how it goes. Things get bad. Then they clear up. Then they get bad again." Yeah, and it happens a lot, Orion thought. He had learned it was the reason that people lived in the urban prairie rather than the city. Gangs had no business there. Yet some schoolhouses and workplaces were close to the boundary, where the residential met the criminal. Orion glanced at his mother. Her face softened and she said, "Kiddo?"

"Yeah?"

"Are you staying home from work today?" she asked.

Orion hesitated. He didn't want to lie. "Well, no…I have to go," he said. "I'll be okay, though. I can defend myself. And they're not out during the day anyway."

She scoffed. "Alright then. I guess I can't tell ya what to do anymore."

"Ma, I'll keep my head on a swivel. I promise." His mother said nothing in response, so Orion turned away. "I better make some breakfast," he said. She feigned a smile before he left the room. Orion hated her guilt trips, but he had been on several of them before. He decided he'd go to work like usual. As he left the room and entered the kitchen, there were loud footsteps on the second-floor stairs. And while he started cracking eggs, the footsteps made it to the kitchen. His brother and cousins shuffled in, yawned, and sat at the table. "Hey," Orion said. He heard no response. While the two kids slumped in their chairs, cousin Mykel joined Orion at the counter.

"Going to work?" he asked. Orion said yes. "Man, that must be nice," Mykel said. "I feel like a damn kid. Staying home because of gangs." He scoffed. "Like that's something new."

"Well, you gotta be safe," Orion said.

"I can defend myself," Mykel said. "And so what? It's not like people get shot outside of a gang." Orion agreed but didn't say anything else. Mykel went on, "You know what? I bet your brother can defend himself. Could probably beat the shit out of a whole gang." He laughed. "The little man can hit hard."

"Derrick's hitting you?"

"Just when we're messing around...with the gloves on. He'll be a great boxer, ya know."

"Yeah, maybe," Orion said. He kept his voice low so the kids couldn't hear. "He's smart, though, and I hope he can get a good education."

"He can't get an education and learn boxing at the same time?" Mykel said. Orion answered and said that he only wanted his brother to keep his focus on school. He didn't want to argue, so he kept quiet and turned his attention to the stove. Mykel helped him fry some old sausage, and they talked about school and work and what Mykel wanted to do when he was out of school. He said he wanted to drop out and get a job in the factory like Orion, but the latter told him not to. Mykel was only 17, and Orion said it was better to stay in school.

"Then maybe you can hope to move out of the city," he said.

When the eggs and sausage were finished, Orion took the last of a bowl of grapes and rationed them out between four plates. He and Mykel brought them to the table and the four of them sat down to eat. Orion figured his mother was either sleeping or doing a crossword puzzle in the other room. It was a rare day that she got up from the bed for more than a couple of hours, and in the winter, it was even less than that. Meanwhile, Derek and Alia were quiet and did not look up. "Hey, look alive," Orion said. "You don't have to go to school. Wish I could be you guys." He nudged his brother and that brought out a smile. But Derek quickly returned to apathy and ate his breakfast. Mykel took the opportunity to joke about a guy in school who claimed the moon wasn't real. He imitated the guy's voice, acting frantic and bug-eyed, as if he was the crazy conspiracist himself. Orion listened and laughed, but he couldn't add anything to the story.

When it was close to 10:00, Orion finished his breakfast, washed the plate, and went to the bedroom he shared with Mykel and his brother. He put on a dark sweater over his flannel and strapped on his work boots, then took a few long strips of electrical tape from the dresser. The zippers on the sides of the boots had broken off years ago, and Orion didn't want to get blisters or have snow get inside the flaps, so he wrapped the tape around each boot, looping it several times to make sure that they stayed tight around his ankle. When he was taped up, Orion pulled a black topcoat from the closet. It was his only coat. His mother didn't like when he wore it because it had belonged to his father. But Orion grew into it and he liked the way it looked. It was single-breasted and long, but not as long as a trench coat. And it fit him so well that it didn't even feel like he was wearing another layer. After throwing the coat on, Orion locked the door and knelt at the edge of the closet. He took a dull pocket knife and drove it into the crack between two floorboards. As he pushed down on the knife, the board popped up and fell onto the floor. Below was a thin space just a few inches across but deep enough to hide two 9mm handguns and a combat knife. After removing the weapons, Orion replaced the floorboard and popped it into place with a firm punch. He took one 9mm and tucked it in the inside pocket of his coat where his right hand could easily reach. He took the other and tucked it under the belt above his rear where his left hand could reach. The combat knife he clipped to his side where it could be quickly drawn, then he draped the coat over it. He was ready to leave. Orion went downstairs and passed straight through the kitchen to the front door. He grabbed his blue knit hat from the counter, then waved and called out, "See y'all." Outside, the sky was overcast and patchy snow was covering the ground. It rested in little blotches everywhere on the grass in empty lots. There were about two or three houses in each block, and the remaining area was urban prairie. The cracks in the street were filled in with snow, so it appeared to be smooth. Orion crossed the street and began to walk along the railroad due east. Ten blocks passed by before the city materialized. It was a 30-minute walk most days, but Orion enjoyed stretching his legs. The air was not as fresh in the city as it was in the neighborhoods, but as long as it was outside air, he didn't mind it. He saw four people along the way, but they were blocks away. Even if they were close, he wouldn't dream of making any sort of contact with them. Most people that were out or going anywhere were probably going to work or school, if they did those things. But that was the extent of it.

City buildings grew taller farther down the rail. Most were empty; picked clean like vulture prey. Between them were shorter structures that were usually factories and mills. They stood with dark brick walls, and most had soot-covered, barred-up windows. Some had been reduced to ruins during the civil war and were rebuilt from abandoned structures and scrap construction materials. The buildings and industry were lifeless, at least on the outside. Orion could hear the sound of machines inside the factories—pounding, coughing, and rum-bling. He didn't know what half of the places produced. There were neither signs nor identifiers to reveal it. Some of them likely made utility materials or appliances for profit. Others were simply a cover-up for opiate operations or manufacturing guns. That was the way it was. Orion worked in one of them. It was an L-shaped factory next to a rundown theater. His boss was a beefy, short-haired man called Creed. He was never sure whether it was the man's first name or last name.

Orion made it to the factory just before 10:45. He en-tered the loading area and glanced inside the building. An old diesel engine powered the clay machine that the factory pretended to operate. Clay was fed to the machine, it was formed, and then crushed and recycled through the machine, over and over again. The engine made a systematic thumping sound. Orion liked the sound because it was tough and consistent. As he watched and waited by the loading area, Creed and his driver, a tall, thin man named John, emerged from the doorway. John offered Orion a cigarette, but the latter declined. "You don't smoke?" John said. Orion told him that he only allowed himself two vices in life: one that would help him be successful and one to help him relax. John replied with a shrug and took a long drag.

"You heard about the Nine O' Two yesterday?" Creed asked.

"Yes, sir," Orion said. "Sounded like they were kind of close to the border."

"The border?"

"The neighborhoods," Orion said. "Corner of the territory. Our territory."

John scoffed. "They're gettin' brave."

"Brave, or maybe just stupid," Creed said. He turned to Orion. "You can ride with Johnny, Devin, and Eric today. I'm going to have them do some runs, so I wanna be safe. What're you packing?"

"Two nines. And I can get that shotgun from your office."

"I wouldn't worry about that. You'll only be out for a few hours. And also…" He reached into his jacket pocket. "…before you leave today, I have a job." He handed Orion a slip of paper with an address and some notes scribbled on it.

Orion read the slip and pocketed it. He nodded and said, "I'll get it taken care of."

"Good," Creed said. "We're going to stay low today. We don't need attention from the Nine O' Two. But if you get into a jam, don't wait to unload on 'em. They should know not to fuck with us." Creed turned to walk out but looked at Orion first. "You're young and you're quick. I trust you to hold your own if you get in a situation?"

"Of course," Orion said. He nodded once and straightened his back. Creed nodded in return, then he walked back into the factory. John muttered something. "What's that?" Orion asked.

"Nine O' Two," John said. "Cutting into our territory? I'd like to put 'em in their place." Orion said he agreed, but he wasn't worried about them. Even in the past, the Nine O' Two rarely crossed his mind.

After a minute, Devin and Eric came walking in from the street. They were both short and had curly, dark hair. The others always joked that they were twins. "Alright, what do we have today?" Eric asked. John told them what Creed wanted, and at that, Eric forced a smile. "Well, ain't it just another day in paradise?" he grinned. As the crew went on with small talk, John brought the truck around. The four men got inside, with Eric in the passenger's seat and Devin in the rear with Orion. The first address took them to the south side of the city where there were several abandoned demolition sites and only small trailers within the borough. John drove to the first few locations, and then the others made pickups of small packages wrapped in paper. Orion scanned every object and structure in the surroundings. At each stop, he stood outside with his back against the car and watched closely as Eric and Devin went inside a trailer and back out within a few seconds. His eyes never left the building, and his right hand was always on the 9mm.

The morning became afternoon, and the sun began to peek out once the pickups were done. John returned to the factory where everyone unloaded the packages and brought them to an empty office room on the second floor. Creed was nowhere in the building, but that wasn't unusual for an afternoon. Orion checked his watch and excused himself from the group. He patted down his coat to make sure the guns were there and checked the paper that Creed gave him. The note read 5:08. Orion's watch showed 4:21. He had some extra time, so he left the factory walking east at a slow pace. The sun was falling in the western half of the sky, its light chopped up and fractured by the skeletal city skyline. The sunlight didn't make the air any warmer, and Orion hated being cold. But he didn't have to worry about it as long as he kept moving. Nothing was ahead except small factories and their muffled, rumbling machinery. The city was comprised entirely of an artificial aliveness. Black clouds rose from each building and covered the area, thick as fog. The smoke drifted through the streets and left dark soot that Orion could see along the walk and sometimes on himself. Nothing was organic. Along the river ahead, there sat an abandoned clinic near a rail yard. Orion had been to it just once; he was born there before it was decommissioned. The clinic was a small building and only three stories tall. It was the next-door neighbor of the rail yard, which made a 90-degree angle near the clinic and went east over the river.

The time was 4:51 when Orion entered the remains of the clinic. He went in through an empty door frame and went down the hall toward the stairs. The walls were covered entirely in graffiti, so much that Orion could barely tell what color they used to be. Some of them were lined with bullet holes and buckshot. There were a few shells scattered on the floor amid the drywall and mangled rebar. Orion looked down through cracks in the staircase where rays of light shot up, revealing the set of stairs below. He carefully walked up the stairwell and went down a similar hall on the second floor. The doors were gone and everything was open. Drafts of cold air blew down the hall and made Orion shiver. Each room had wide and empty window frames. The noise of the surrounding industry was somewhat muted inside the clinic, making it hauntingly silent. Orion imagined he was walking through the carcass of a giant. One of the rooms he passed looked out over the rail yard, and it was perfectly in line with the bridge. Orion went inside and gazed out the empty windowsill. The ground was only a short jump below, where a muddy embankment was built up against the first floor. It would be the perfect spot for him. There was a tattered box spring along the wall, so Orion sat down. He could look to his left and see where the rail yard turned east toward the bridge. It was 4:55. Orion took a few deep breaths. The air near the river seemed to be a little bit cleaner. There was no smoke. Even though it was in the core of the city, there was an atmosphere of peace. But not wanting to drift off, Orion kept his eyes open. He looked out at the rail yard and watched the sun pouring through the building. He felt the breeze washing through and listened to the distant rumbling of machines.

It was 5:01 and Orion was caught in a reverie. He glanced around and focused on the railroad below. The sun was almost setting, and the breeze picked up only slightly. He stood up and paced the room to stay warm. He sat back down. His watch showed the time at 5:04. Down the rail line, a small gray engine was coming slowly and pulling three boxcars. Orion leaned back and waited. As the engine grew closer to the bend, Orion could hear its chugging. It rounded the turn slowly. The boxcars followed behind, and there was the shriek of grinding steel on the tracks. The engine slowed just a little bit. The front of it was nearly around the bend. Orion decided to move. Climbing over the empty windowsill, he turned his back to the railroad and scaled halfway down the wall. He hopped off and fell into a roll down the embankment. Springing up, Orion dashed across the embankment. Upon the rail yard, there was the sound of grinding brakes. The engine noise was quieting. Orion crossed the embankment around the bend and jumped onto a support beam that angled upward. He ran up it, holding his arms straight out at his side to keep his balance. The beam stopped just under a guard rail, so he latched onto it with both hands and lifted himself up and onto the rail yard. The engine was on the farthest set of tracks, idling and spitting black smoke. Orion ran toward it, this time a little slower and lighter on his feet. He made sure to stay behind the engine and within its blind spot. He jogged until he was behind the engine and right next to the first boxcar. A foggy rear window revealed a silhouette still inside. This was the man. He was probably ready to leave the train at any moment to make his delivery, and Orion didn't want to catch the man out in the open. So, he stepped across the link between the engine and the boxcar and approached. There was a doorway on the side of the engine. This was it. Orion reached into his coat, drew his gun, and jumped into the cabin. The man stepped off to the side and made a startled yell. Orion fired twice at point-blank, directly into the heart. The man's look of shock faded to lifelessness. He fell backward and crumpled to the floor of the cabin. Silence followed. It was backed only by white noise from the engine. The man did not have a second of life left to cry out in pain. Orion lowered his gun and sighed. He turned and noticed a small package wrapped in brown paper sitting on the control board. He picked it up, returning the 9mm to his coat pocket. The package felt heavy enough to be the thing Creed was looking for, so Orion put it in his left pocket then looked to the control board. After some guessing, he was able to find and release the brake. Then he took the throttle and cranked it as far as it would go. The engine roared and Orion hopped out of the cabin. Blood began to drip down from the doorway. Orion stood by and watched as the train picked up momentum and the boxcars slowly rumbled past. The fading sunlight felt warm on his cheek as he stood. He wondered how old the man was. He figured he couldn't have been more than 30. He had thick hair and a young face. Reaching into his right pocket, Orion felt the folded stack of dollar bills there. Creed had given it to him just an hour ago. There was over one grand there. It was enough to feed the family with decent food and then some. Orion had already been saving his surplus with the thought of the family moving away one day. He had a lot of money already, but it would take more, maybe six months' worth. Even then, there was always a contingency—they could be robbed, caught in a gunfight, or fail to find a decent place to settle. But anywhere else was certainly nicer than the city, Orion figured. It had to be.

The train was gone in seconds, chugging its way to God-knows-where with a dead passenger. Orion turned toward the sun and started to walk. He was feeling hungry, and it was time to go home.

June of the Rust Belt

WHEN HE WAS ONLY 21, my friend Clark claimed a house on the east side of the river. After the revolution, it was easy to come across abandoned houses. No bank was there to claim it, nor was anyone there to transfer the deed. So, Clark held his house for two years, and I lived in it with him when I was 22. It was a red-brick Queen Anne home, and it had an added second-floor balcony and a garage that was converted into a bedroom. Clark called it his "mansion," but it was really just a big house. I knew Clark from school. He was a friendly guy, short but athletic, and I liked him. We hung out every day when we were in school, and afterward he would walk to our house to visit me and help my mom as she cooked us supper. She loved the hell out of him and thought he was the sweetest person in the world. Later, when he heard about my mom leaving, he said that I could move into his house and stay as long as I wanted to. He knew a lot of people who lost their parents to the work camps, and so did I. Four of us lived in the house then.

It was me, Clark, Camile, and Michael. I had the garage bedroom to myself for the first few months. And when they weren't sleeping with each other, which seemed to happen at random times, Clark and Camile had their own rooms on the second floor. Michael slept alone and worked in the guest bedroom. To keep us all fed, Clark, Michael, and Camile ran a business selling vegetables. The sunroom functioned as a greenhouse filled wall-to-wall with cucumbers, butter lettuce, spinach, and tomatoes. Sometimes we'd grow strawberries, which were rare around the neighborhood. People would usually hand over a good chunk of their savings just to get a taste of them. All of us helped grow the food, and Clark and Camile would sell it at the market a few blocks away, as well as old, abandoned bicycles that Clark found—or said he found—and would repair by himself in the empty attic. Michael was in charge of the money, so he kept a detailed list of what we had to sell and what we needed to buy every week. He was meticulous and sometimes got mad at Clark for miscounting. Michael hated wasting and spending any more than what we needed to spend. I couldn't blame him. We made just enough to survive.

I moved into Clark's just before summer, after my mom had been shipped off to a corporate work camp to pay off the family's debt. She had told me, "Don't worry, hon, it'll only be six months and then I'll be home, and maybe they'll even let us keep the house." But I didn't believe her. I had heard of people's parents who went to work camps and either died of malnourishment or came out a year later, exhausted and back-broken to the point of being crippled. So, I cried the tears I had to cry and told mom that I hoped it was just a few months and that I'd think of her every day. Then I was alone. And I did think of her every day, just like I did with dad. The new ruling class couldn't have taken my dad away because he was already dead. The revolution wasn't kind to him. It wasn't to a lot of others either. My uncle was the only true revolutionary in our family, and he couldn't stand my disagreeing dad, but it didn't matter. In the end, the revolution failed, and corporations began taking over amid the hurricane of rebellion and anarchy. Right from the beginning, my dad couldn't get on board with the revolution, yet he stood by Uncle Mike anyway, refusing to step away from the door when the armament came to his house to take him. My uncle was a revolutionary, but he never hurt anyone. And my dad left this life defending that honor. I didn't know where Uncle Mike had gone, but I knew he was kept alive by my dad, at least for a while. I hoped my uncle was doing well. I hoped he woke up every day thinking of his brother and how he saved him.

The first couple of months at Clark's were quiet on my part. I spent most of them running. When I was younger, I had started running because dad did. He would push me along in a stroller for hours and hours until I was old enough to run a few miles or so, then we'd go out together, exploring every suburb and riverwalk from one side of the city to the other. Then I just kept going and ran cross country at school for six years, training with dad every week in the offseason. After the revolution and after mom left, I was on my own, and then I realized that I didn't just enjoy running—I needed to run. I needed to feel the wind in my face and feel the earth and the grass rushing underneath me; nothing able to hold me down. I could go anywhere I wanted and never stop. It was the most freedom anyone could have in a world locked in post-revolution limbo. Clark hated it though, and he let me know every time he'd catch me coming back after a run, which was at least a few times a week. "June, I love ya," he'd say, "but c'mon. Going out by yourself? It's not like it used to be out there…it's getting more and more dangerous. Ya gotta stop." I always gave him the same answer: "I'll run faster next time." Clark would scoff at that and go back to his bike room. And in the morning, I'd lace up my old racing flats and head out the door. It was always the same.

When summer officially came and every day was greeted with a warm bath of sunshine, I ran every morning, working my mileage up to the double digits so that I could spend a few hours running every day. Since I was gone most mornings of the week, Clark gave up fighting me on it. Instead, he'd be passive-aggressive, ignoring me and avoiding eye contact as soon as I'd come back. I was usually too tired, hot, and sweaty to care. With some rest, I could sit and wonder how mom was doing and whether or not dad was looking over us, and then I'd move on to think about how much Clark pissed me off. I'd build up a bit of resentment and burn most of that energy running the next day. Clark and I continued being friendly to each other, but our conversations were only a sentence or two before we'd go on our separate ways, not wanting to exhaust ourselves bickering again. It was easier to be cold and isolated. Still, whenever I finished a run early, I'd join Clark, Camile, and Michael at the market. I liked getting out on nice days, and Camile and I would usually kick back at the market and crack jokes as Clark went around the other tables and tried to be a salesman. It was hard to sell bikes because there wasn't much demand, and his in-your-face sales tactics didn't help. Still, the vegetables made us our money, and as long as we'd leave with a profit, then Michael would give us a thumbs-up of approval.

One blistering Thursday, I ended my run early and still felt a lot of pent-up energy, so I told Clark and Camile I would help them at the market. Michael was staying in to sleep off a cold. He usually pulled the wagon, Clark said, so I volunteered to take his place. "Let's get this thing on the road before it gets any hotter," Clark said. "Whew! I swear those tomatoes are gonna cook themselves out there." I noticed that Clark's wintertime beanie had transitioned to a floral bandana, which held back the waves of his thick, brown hair. He always had some kind of hat or bandana on his head. I thought he was attractive, and he had a nice smile, but I couldn't stand to look at his headwear. I never liked bandanas on guys. Dad never wore one that I could remember, and that was fine. I didn't like seeing it on Clark, and having to look at it more and more, I started to hate it. When I did talk to him, I'd look down at his nose or his chin so I wouldn't have to stare at his bandana. He must've truly loved it to be wearing it all the time. So, I didn't say anything about it and just let him do his thing.

We left the house and I pulled the wagon topped with veggies as Camile trailed behind. Clark used both of his hands to steer a pair of bikes. "Careful with these potholes, man," he said. "Hit a big one and the cucumbers will go flying." I told him I would and shut my mouth. Camile kept a hand on the top of the pile to steady it, and we continued up the hill. The market was in a roundabout. Sellers like us set up their tables around the concrete circle, displaying apples and grapes, vegetables, fresh chicken and beef, T-shirts and shoes, and a scattering of old cooking utensils. The tables on the roundabout all faced inward toward the big trailer that sat in the grassy patch at the center. It was a covered semi-trailer that never moved. There was a single aisle down the middle of it, and its walls were lined with shelves of soap, toiletries, cups, plates, and canned vegetables and broth. The person who ran it was a middle-aged bald man who was always so busy organizing and stocking the shelves that you couldn't talk to him for more than a second. He'd only answer in short bursts: "Back and second shelf from bottom." "Top shelf. Next to towels." "Toilet paper? Two dollars." He had everything in that trailer, and there were always hordes of people walking through. I couldn't imagine how much money the guy made. Busy people like him were the biggest earners, from what I could tell. The art of making money didn't allow for small talk or downtime.

We locked the wheels of our wagon and sat down on the curb as Clark propped up his bikes and stood by them, lean-

ing one arm against the crossbar as if he were part of the display—a package deal. Camile looked at me, giggled, and shook
her head. "Would you pay fifty bucks for a bike?" she asked.

"Not Clark's," I said.

We took care of a few buyers and sat back again as people
would walk past. They were an entire spectrum. Our neighborhood didn't discriminate because it couldn't. Almost everyone
was poor after the revolution, no matter who they were or what
they looked like. At the market, there were families with little kids, squads of estranged young adults like us, old couples,
middle-aged couples, and the occasional single man or woman
keeping to themselves and gathering a backpack full of supplies
to take home alone. There was a little grove behind us, and as
the sun moved west, it provided a little shade over our stretch of
the curb. Camile sighed and put her hair up. She had the lon-
gest hair I'd ever seen. It was down to her waist then, and the
slightest breeze would toss the front of it in her face. I would get
sweaty just looking at her and imagining all of that hair smoth-
ering me while I ran. I kept my own hair in cornrows most of
the time, clipped at the back to keep the thick of it off my neck.
I never did anything special with it, but I always felt good because Camile said I shouldn't worry about how it looked. She
thought it was beautiful the way I had it.

Clark returned to the wagon with a handful of cash. He
unfolded the bills and showed them to us. It was $60. "One
bike sold, one to go," he grinned. He handed Camile a few of
the bills and stuffed the rest into his pocket. He told us to pick

up some eggs while he watched the wagon, so we headed off with the cash. There was a woman at the market who owned a house nearby, and she often brought her chickens with her. They'd roam around the market, picking at things in the grass and bobbing their heads as they walked down the road. Sometimes they'd get irritated and peck at the legs of a startled passerby. Then everyone nearby would laugh and go about their business. Everyone loved the lady who owned them. Her name was Anita, and she was simple and overly kind. Every week or so, she'd give us a free dozen just because we'd listen to her talk. She was bent over a pallet stacked with egg cartons, a bandana around her head as if she were a 1950s housewife. Camile said good morning and she immediately turned around.

"Well, hey there! How are my lovelies today? Need restocking?"

"Yep," I said. "We go through 'em so quick."

"I understand, I understand," she said. She pulled a carton from the top of the pallet, inspected it, and handed it to me. "Do you want two?" she asked. "I'll give ya another for free if you think you need it."

"We'll be okay," Camile said. "You've already given us a lot."

"Well, alrighty then," Anita said. "Lotta people think they don't need 'em, then boom, it's Wednesday and they don't have any eggs left. Now, especially, people aren't coming to the market as much anymore. They're afraid to leave home. I am too, to be honest." She gently tapped her waistband. "That's why I have this on me all the time." I couldn't see what it was because she had an apron around her waist, but I assumed it was a knife. It probably wasn't a gun. I didn't know many people who could manage to get one.

"Have you had any problems?" Camile asked. I was ready to leave and wrap up the conversation, but I didn't say anything.

"No, thank God," Anita said. "I had some furniture robbed last month though, but it happened at night and I was sleeping. Woke up in the morning and my whole living room was gone. Window shattered all across the floor. So, I sleep with this thing now." She tapped her waistband again. "You never know which of 'em might want to hurt you and which ones just want your valuables. Some of 'em are crazy, you know. I used to know a woman who'd come to the market a lot, and we'd talk about our animals and whatnot. She lived a little further down from me. Anyway, I stopped seeing her after a while. I walked by her house one day, and there were two young men standing on the porch. One of 'em had a pistol strapped to his hip."

"Are you thinking they…?"

"I hope not," Anita said. "I really, really hope not. But it wouldn't be unheard of. That's how some people work. Preying on defenseless old folks like us, and basically taking their place in the world, living in their homes. It's not worth the elites' time to police it. 'Let the public go about their business,' I guess. 'They'll work it out themselves and it's not our problem.'" Camile just shook her head. I thought for a moment and figured criminals like that wouldn't try to overthrow a house of four young people. They couldn't. It would be too risky. If we had weapons, they wouldn't know what all we were packing.

We thanked Anita and went back to the wagon, where Clark was counting what stock we had left. The remaining bike was still there. "We'll take home a week's worth of veggies and an average amount of profit, it looks like," Clark said. He told us he was going to pick up some pawpaw plants and came back with a single pot with a sprout in it, and then we were off. The market was quieting down, and a few dark clouds were growing larger in the western sky. They were far-off, but we walked fast anyway and didn't talk. I sat down on the porch and watched the clouds while Camile cleared out the wagon and Clark took a nap. After a few minutes, Camile came outside. She didn't say anything at first and sat down, taking in a few deep breaths. There was the sound of thunder in the distance. I leaned my head back against the wall and sighed. It was beginning to smell like rain. I wanted to break the silence but hesitated. I waited a second and the question came out on its own.

"So, what's going on with you and Clark?" I asked.

Camile smirked. "I don't know, really."

"You've been hooking up as long as I've lived here," I said, keeping my voice low.

"Well, off and on," Camile said. "Yeah. You know Clark. He's a great guy. I think he wants it to happen, but I'm just not sure. It doesn't feel right to be together in this kind of world, you know? At the same time, I just can't help myself being really attracted to him. It's not good, I know, but I deal with it. I try putting my foot down, at least."

"Have you told him all of this?" I asked. Camile nodded. She kept quiet then, so I stopped asking questions. I didn't actually care about her business with Clark anyway. It was starting to rain and I was feeling tired now, cooked from the sun we soaked up at the market.

"What do you think Anita was packing under that apron?" Camile asked.

"I don't know," I said. "Probably a knife. Like a combat knife or something."

Camile smiled. "I can just picture her waving that thing around to defend herself." She swung an imaginary knife wildly from side to side. "You know how feisty Anita would be. She doesn't take shit from nobody."

"She'd probably sic her chickens on 'em," I said. We both laughed at that.

Camile sighed. "Speaking of which, do you take anything with you when you go on your runs?" I figured she was talking about a weapon, but I still asked her what she meant. "I don't know," she said. "Mace? A knife? Anything like that?" I told her no. Camile nodded and there was a pause. "You don't?" she said. "If I were going out like that all the time, I might carry something. It'd just make me feel better, just having it, you know?"

"Well, you don't run as fast as I do," I joked.

Camile didn't laugh. She continued like she didn't hear me. "Actually, if I were you, I might not go out at all," she said. "And not just because I hate running."

"Yeah, but I want to," I said. "Especially now, since I'd go crazy here."

"Why's that?"

"Clark," I said, sighing. "He won't let me go out for even ten minutes without bitching about it. And now you're on my case."

"Sorry, I didn't mean it to come off like I was bitching at you," Camile said. "You know, we just don't want anything to happen to you. It's scary out there."

I told her I knew that already and said, "My dad is dead and my mom is at a work camp 'til God knows when. They didn't go out running around the city every day. So, what does it matter? You're fucked no matter what you do."

"That's not true," Camile said. "I think you're just using it as an excuse to go out and run and blow off steam. It's just a distraction. I think I know you well enough to tell."

"What does that mean? Are you my mom all of a sudden?" I said. "What do you care?"

Camile scoffed and shook her head. She leaned back and wiped at her eyes, staring straight ahead at the sky. "You think I don't understand?" she said. "It was the exact same for me. I couldn't deal with being on my own; no family. But I didn't run like you. Huh. No, I drank every day. Drank everything in my sight until the house was dry. Then I went out and bought more the next day. I didn't do anything else for a month until Clark dragged me out of my room and made me help him start gardening. And eventually, I wasn't living in hell anymore."

The door suddenly opened and Clark stepped out onto the porch before stopping, hand still on the door. "Everything alright?" he asked.

"Ask June," Camile said.

Clark looked at me. "What's the matter?" he asked. He glanced back at Camile.

"Nothing," she said, wiping her eye again.

Clark looked at me, brow furrowed. "Hey look," he said, "we don't want to have a house in disorder. So, what's up?"

I sighed, telling him what Camile had said to me and that I didn't want to hear it from him again either. I looked him in the eye and said, "I can take care of myself. End of discussion."

Clark stared at me for a second then shook his head. "Okay," was all he said. Camile repeated to him what she claimed about my running being a distraction. Clark nodded. "You know, I've been saying this forever," he said. "I'm not going to repeat myself. You know what we think."

"I'm only responsible for myself," I said. "Stop trying to… to make this about you. It's not."

"We never said it was."

"Then why won't you let it go? Why won't you let me go?"

"Because it's really about you," Camile said. "God knows what could happen to you, spending so many hours out in this…mess of a city. There are psychopaths out there. People robbing. Rapists. Human traffickers. And I'd say the same thing to Clark or Michael if it was one of them running." I didn't want to hear Camile say anymore, so I didn't respond to her.

"We've got to look out for each other," Clark said. "That's all Camile is saying. I mean, what else do we have? I stopped going out at night after I was mugged. Remember I told you about that last month? Couldn't sleep for like, weeks. Just…we have to be smart, that's all."

"Maybe you're right," I said. "Maybe I'm just the dumb one in this group." I stood up and grabbed the door.

Camile looked up and asked, "Where are you going?" I didn't say anything, letting the door close behind me. Neither of them followed me inside, so I went into my room and shut the door; stood in front of my bed. For a second, I wondered what Camile was like before I moved in. Her parents were both dead. And Clark, Michael, and I were just estranged. I wanted to cry but fought the tears and didn't. I lay on the bed until the window went dark, and I waited to fall asleep, not knowing what time it was for several hours.

In the morning, I woke up and the room was full of loud, squeaking chirps. I could've sworn that whatever kind of bird it was had been sitting at the foot of my bed. I took a pillow and threw it above my head against the window. There was the flapping of wings and the chirps faded away. The pillow fell back down on top of my head, so I let it rest there and slept for another few minutes before starting to sweat under the sheets. This time, I got up and put on my shorts and racing flats, then headed into the kitchen to make a little breakfast. As the eggs fried, I filled a half-gallon milk jug with water and drank from it. Michael came into the kitchen as I sat down and ate. He was tall and skinny and was always wearing a cutoff T-shirt. He kept to himself most of the time. Before he opened the cabinet, he saw me at the table and said, "Hey."

"Hey," I said. "How are you? I didn't see you yesterday."

"Yeah, I felt like a hell for a while. Sort of better now, though. Clark got me some cough medicine, so that's been helping."

"That's good," I said. I glanced at my watch and noticed it was almost 10:00. Usually, Clark was up and around by 8:00. "Where are they, by the way?" I asked.

"They went over to Anita's," Michael said. "I guess she had some work to do in her garden. She was going to pay them for it." I nodded and then finished breakfast, sitting back in the chair in silence. "Are you alright?" Michael asked.

"Yeah, I'm fine," I said. Then I sighed and asked, "Hey, can I ask you a question?"

"Yeah, what's up?"

"So, in the past few months, have you heard from your parents at all?"

Michael shook his head. He sighed. "Well, actually, I did once," he said. "That was like a couple weeks after they were sent away. Didn't say much, just a short little letter about how they loved me and missed me. Said they were doing alright, but I'm not sure I really believed it. It was my mom's handwriting for sure, but it didn't sound at all like something she'd say." He shook his head again and said, "I don't think she came up with that note herself." He looked up at me. "Have you?"

"No," I said. "It's been about a month." Michael nodded.

"Does it bother you?" I asked.

"Of course."

"You don't really show it," I said.

"Well, I guess I've just accepted it," he said. "Not much we can do, you know? I hope I'll see them again next year, and I'm sure I will. But there's nothing I can do to make it get here any faster."

"I get what you mean, but you're just so calm about it. I mean, I think about my mom breaking her back out there and it makes me want to break into that camp and just burn the whole place down. I don't know how I can sit here another day without going insane."

"I get it," Michael said. "You know me, I'm pretty passive, so it's just easier for me. But honestly, it really wasn't for a while. I was depressed and couldn't get out of my bed for more than a couple hours a day."

"Did Clark have to drag you out of bed, too? Camile said he forced her to start gardening with him."

"They both dragged me out of bed," Michael laughed. "They'd have to come into my room and throw the sheets off, blasting music through the house until I'd get up."

"God," I said. "I'd be so mad."

Michael shrugged. "I mean, it worked," he said. "And at least they played good songs."

I smiled at that. "Well, that's a matter of opinion," I said. "Me and Clark have had some debates about what good music is."

"Oh, I can imagine," Michael said. "Where did you get your music taste from? Your parents?"

"Yeah," I said. "My mom and dad were pretty much into the same stuff. There was a lot of old-school soul played in our house. Honestly, a lot of everything else, too—80s pop, even, 90s pop, old dance music. My dad had this big stereo in the living room that my mom got for him when I was little." In my head, I could hear the sound of dad's six-CD changer whirring and clicking as it changed from the grand, powerful voice of Jackie Wilson to snare-heavy beats of new jack swing.

"I wish I had had the chance to meet your dad," Michael said. "He seemed like the most wholesome person."

"He was," I said. "But he wasn't always that way."

"Really?"

"Yeah," I said, "he was an alcoholic before I was born. And before he met my mom, he'd been in and out of prison for several years, after getting drunk and getting in fights. He even stabbed my uncle one time they were fighting outside his house. Eventually, he got it together one day and decided to get an apartment and a job. And at some point, he met my mom. She must've seen a calmer side to him that she liked. I guess then he quit drinking after they started dating and… here we are. And thankfully, he made up with Uncle Mike. They weren't best friends, but they had a much better under-standing than before."

"You told me how he defended your uncle," Michael said. "I think he more than redeemed himself."

"Yes," I said. "I'm glad he did it because he was a great man and that just proved it. It was just one of the things, really. But it also sucks. Life just sucks without him in it." I sighed. "And since my mom was taken, I just can't deal with it. It's like life was just laughing in my face at that point; sticking a knife in my chest and twisting it. I still think that."

"You have every right to," Michael said.

"Maybe," I said. "But I look at Camile. She lost both her parents within a month of each other. Considering that, my situation is nothing."

"It's not nothing," Michael said. "It's something. We all have our something. You just have to accept it for what it is, you know? Only that. That's the hardest part, really. But look at Camile...she did it."

"I think I know what you tried to say there," I said, "but how? Does it just happen magically that one day you stop caring about what happened?"

"Well, no, I don't think it's like that," Michael said. "No one can stop caring. Not completely, I don't think."

"Then what do you mean?"

"You love your parents. You love your mom. A lot," Michael said. "But you can't see her right now. And you don't know what's going to happen. Neither do I. We don't know when we'll see them again. That's just a fact, and so I've realized that. I've accepted it as a fact." He looked down. "Huh," he said. "You know, it's easy to do when you have no other choice." I was watching and listening in silence, and he must have noticed. He met my gaze and continued, "But here's another fact. I've realized this: I'm here now, at this moment, with you and Clark and Camile, and that's all right. Don't get me wrong, I want to see my parents more than anything. God, I really do. But if I can look around and see you guys here with me every day, plugging along just like I'm trying to…then maybe I'm doing fine." I told him, all things considered, he was doing better than fine. "We all are," he said. "You know, sometimes it helps if I just look around me." He pointed up at the ceiling and then around the room. "Because this…" he said, "…this is all that there is."

"I can't tell you you're wrong," I said. "It's true. This is what it is." He smiled, his eyes tired and starting to droop, and said that he was going to lie down for a while. He stood up and headed for the stairs. My head was full of one, endless philosophical thought now, so I went to the front door to run but stopped before opening it. "I hope you feel better," I called out.

Michael turned around for a second and said, "Thanks, June." The stairs creaked as he walked up and faded out of sight. Then I was out the door. I started running as soon as I reached the porch stairs. It was cloudy outside and the air was humid and thick, so I struggled to find a good pace, moving like I was trying to run through a pool. Less than a minute passed and I couldn't get out of the funk, having to use all my effort to move forward. So, I stopped at the end of the block and stood at the curb, taking a few deep breaths. I glanced back at our empty house. It was stark and washed-out under the gray sky. A darker cloud was hanging above it in the southern sky, and it seemed to be moving closer. Westward, near the market and Anita's house, the neighborhood was still and quiet. Clark and Camile were there, I figured, hard at work without me. I thought about it and wanted to see them. A couple of gusts of wind drifted through the trees overhead, and I realized I'd have to run fast to make it to Anita's before it got worse and the rain hit. So, I turned on my heel and picked up my pace, heading up the street toward the end of the quiet boulevard. A minute later, I was at the market roundabout, which was then a circle of empty asphalt with only the locked-up trailer sitting motionless in the center. I ran up to it and around it, heading straight down the street on the other side.

When I reached Anita's block, there were a few random raindrops falling. I ran faster, zooming up the sidewalk toward Anita's little brick ranch and stopping at the edge of her yard to catch my breath and walk up to the door. No birds were chirping and the wind was starting to blow through the maple trees that draped over the house at every corner. A rush of wind blew a few stray leaves past my head, and then I was on the porch in front of the door. I heard a deep shout from inside the house. With my hand on the doorknob, I stopped. I looked through the screen door and saw Clark, Camile, and Anita up against the far wall of the kitchen, lined up shoulder-to-shoulder. Standing in front of them were two people with their backs to me. The strangers wore bright-colored gaiters around their mouths and one of them waved a long knife in front of him. I could see it gleam in the light as it moved back and forth and came into view. They were speaking to the other three, but I couldn't hear anything. Clark went silent after a moment, and I could see that the color had drained from his face. One of the captors said something and started to move toward Clark, raising his knife. Clark began to put his hands up in front of him in defense. My heart jumped and my hand tightened around the door handle. The next moment lasted maybe one second, but I felt it happening in slow-motion like I was stuck in a bad action movie. Clark looked up and saw me as I swung the door open. His mouth slowly opened into a shout. I was already halfway through the kitchen. Clark's attacker turned and was ready to meet me, arm raised straight up toward the ceiling with the knife bearing down. I stared into a pair of bright blue eyes above the guy's mask, then we collided. I felt a burning and the cold sting of metal sinking itself deep inside my shoulder. I wanted to scream but couldn't and made a pained growl instead. There was shouting at the other end of the room and a couple of crashes that sounded like dishes breaking. I backed up for a moment and felt the blade slide out of my arm. The guy lowered his knife this time and winded up, ready to strike straight forward into my heart. I caught his arm with mine and pushed it upward, along with the knife, throwing my body weight into him. Then I moved my right leg behind his left and tripped him from behind, still pushing against his chest. The combination of the trip and the push threw him off balance so much that he went horizontal for a moment and we fell to the ground. His head was the first thing to hit the floor, and it bounced at least once before his body hit and I came down on top of him. The knife flew backward and I heard the grating sound of it sliding across the hardwood, but I was still down and couldn't see anything. The guy made a soft groan. He was limp underneath me and apparently dazed. I heard Clark say something, and then a pair of arms lifted me to my feet. The one arm around my shoulder pushed into the wet, bloody gash, and the white-hot burning spread from my clavicle to the skin of my back. I shouted and tried to plant my feet and stand up straight. "Grab it! Grab it!" a voice shouted. I looked up to see Camile pick up the knife that had hit the wall. She held it above her head, towering over the attacker who was on all fours now, moving slowly and putting a hand up to surrender. Clark appeared and grabbed him by the arm and pulled him to his feet. Then I noticed the second knife in Clark's other hand. He pulled the gaiter down from the guy's mouth and looked him in the eye. The guy had soft, pale cheeks and looked like he was no more than a teenager.

"It's over, alright?" Clark said. "Stay out of this neighborhood!" He pushed the boy away. "Get out! Get the fuck out of here!" The attacker was already stumbling toward the door and as soon as he opened it, he sprinted down the sidewalk and disappeared from view. Clark went to the door and watched to make sure the boy was gone. He still held the knife up near his chest with a tense grip; his knuckles white. Camile took a washcloth from the kitchen and put it against my cut.

"Did it slice all the way through?" Anita asked. She glanced at the back of my shirt.

"I don't think so," I said. Camile told me to sit down, so I did, leaning back against the counter.

"I can't believe you," Anita said. "You've got some guts." She washed out the cut, which only made the burning hotter, then she gave me some ibuprofen and the last of an old bottle of vodka and went to get her suture kit. "I was an ER nurse not too long ago," she assured me.

"Before the revolution?" I asked.

"Before the revolution."

I lay down and Anita's suture didn't take too long, nor was it too painful. All I could feel was the burning inside my shoulder, deep below the skin. As the painkillers set in, the burning went down a couple of degrees, but not many. Every minute or so, I would see Clark look away from the window and glance down at me. Anita saw him watching and said, "You'll have to get her some antibiotics from someone at the market. I have some amoxycillin I can give ya, but it won't be enough to last." Clark nodded. He was silent and went back to looking out the door. Anita shook her head while she continued working, and she kept saying "those sons of bitches" over and over again. "I'm going to stay at Rose's for a while," she said. "She's got her kids there and no one'd ever dare mess with that family. Their breed is tough." She shook her head again and continued, "In broad daylight now. It's sad what's happening, and I'm thinking it will only get worse. Ugh. What are we gonna do? Didn't think

I'd need to keep my knife on me while I'm just working around the house. But here we are." Anita helped me up to a sitting position, then she went upstairs to pack a suitcase.

"You know, I don't know about the market anymore," Camile said. "I don't know how I feel about going, even if it's during the day."

"We're all picking up weapons," Clark said. "I'll talk to my buddy and see if he has any pistols to sell. That'd be best. Strength in numbers is what we need. We don't want this…" He nodded in my direction. "…to happen to anyone again." I didn't say anything. He was right. Camile still stood by the counter with the knife tight in her hand. When Anita returned with a single suitcase, Clark said he would walk with her to Rose's house. "And we'll walk damn fast," he said. Anita agreed and before she told us goodbye, she handed me some of the amoxycillin. I swallowed the tablets dry. Then she and Clark were gone, walking west, and Camile and I headed east down the same street. A cool rain sprinkled on us and I kept one hand on my shoulder, trying not to swing my arm as we walked.

"Well, this sucks," I said. "I won't be able to run for a long time."

Camile smiled. "We'll take care of you," she said. "You'll be back on your feet soon."

We got back to the house and as soon as we were in the door, Michael couldn't stop asking questions. "Are you alright? Were you mugged? Wait…where's Clark? Do we need to leave?" Camile told him to relax and go get some water, so he rushed into the kitchen and came back with my half-gallon jug. I drank what water was left and Michael went back to refill it. Camile took me up to her room and I rested on her bed while she took an old linen sheet and cut it up to make a new bandage.

"Don't want you getting blood on my pillow," Camile said.

I laughed. "That's your main concern right now?"

Camile laughed. "Obviously," she said.

I lay back on the bed and fell asleep for a few minutes, slowly waking to the drumming of rain on the roof. It was humid but cool in the room, and I felt a draft coming from the cracked window. I stared through it at rain pattering down on the topmost leaves of the tree there. Then I saw Clark in the corner of my eye. He was sitting quietly in the corner of the room, legs hunched up and arms folded over them. As I started to move onto my back, he got up and walked over to the bed. "Need anything?" he asked. I said a drink would be good. He handed me the jug and I took a few sips. "That was probably the dumbest, bravest thing I've ever seen," he said. "I still can't believe it." He dragged a milkcrate out from under Camile's bed and sat down next to me.

"How's Anita?" I asked.

"Ah," he sighed. "She's okay. Rose is a good person. She'll be fine there. Honestly, she was just an easy target for them. I'm sure it's their goal to target older people like her. Older people living alone."

"It's funny," I said.

"What's funny?"

"At the market yesterday, she was talking about a lady she knew that went missing. Same deal. She lived alone."

"Well, thank God that wasn't her today," Clark said. "The world would be just that much worse without Anita in it."

"I agree."

"Well, I hope you'd agree," he said. "I mean, you did save her life today."

"Nah," I said. "I'm sure she would've fought those two herself."

Clark shook his head. "No," he said. "All three of us were scared. I was...well, I was preparing myself to die at that moment." He looked away, almost in shame. I let him think in silence for a little bit.

Eventually, I asked, "What were they there for?"

"Just to steal what Anita had," Clark said. "One of them was going to guard us while the other got whatever they were going to get. But then the short guy convinced the other one they couldn't leave us as witnesses."

"Why? Did you know them?"

"No. He just wanted us out of the way, I guess. It's easy to do when there's no justice system. I just have a bad feeling this is turning into the new normal." He paused, then said, "So why did you do that? I have to know. Why'd you charge them?"

"Any of you would've done the same," I said. "I mean, you fought the one guy and got the knife from him, too."

"Yeah, but just seconds before I was honestly ready to piss my pants," Clark said. "I just jumped at the opportunity once you startled them. You took a dagger to the shoulder for me."

"And Camile," I said. "And Anita."

"Of course," Clark said. He laughed, "Let's be honest, you probably didn't want to save me. I've been a dick. Telling you off for running every day."

"You were a little bit right, though," I said. I nodded down at the bedsheet wrapped around my shoulder. "I mean, I was sort of on a run when it happened."

"That might be true, but I was the one who needed to be more careful," Clark said. He sighed. "I'm sorry for being so controlling. I know it really bothered you."

"It's okay," I said.

"I'll never go anywhere again without some kind of defense," he went on. "You shouldn't have to have been stabbed just because of me. Or because of us, I guess."

"It's not the worst thing that's ever happened to me," I said. "I'd take more than one stab to the shoulder to see my mom and dad again."

"Same here," Clark said. "I miss 'em. And your mom, too. She always made me happy. Singing in the kitchen. Feeding me raw cookie dough." He smiled. "And your dad. He's proud of you. I know he is."

"No, not at all," I said. I hadn't done anything worthy of pride.

Clark dismissed me, shaking his head. "You're just like him," he said. "Stubborn, yes. Opinionated, yes. But determined. And tough. I'm sure he's looking down and smiling and wondering what the hell you're still doing hanging out with a guy like me."

I had started to cry, but then I laughed. "He'd never say it, but he respected you," I said. "He was just too..."

"...Too much like you," Clark said.

"Yeah, that's fair," I said, sighing. "I'm sorry."

"For what?"

"Being so stubborn."

"Don't be sorry for that, it's who you are. I made you feel worse than you already did by being controlling."

"You didn't mean to be controlling," I said.

Clark shrugged. "I guess you're right, but either way, I won't bug you anymore. Let's leave it in the past, huh?" I said yes, of course. Clark put his hand on my good arm. "We're going to be all right," he said. "We're going to be fine. In a few months, we're going to see our parents walking up the drive. We'll have supper together and play cards or something, and it'll be like nothing ever happened." Thinking about that made me smile. I told Clark I'd hold him to that. "Noted," he said. "I don't know how your mom would feel about it, though. Seeing me again."

"Oh, shut up, you know she loves you," I said. Clark laughed and said he was joking.

As the sun went down, Camile and Michael came into the room and we all listened to music for a few hours, half playing euchre and half telling stories about the times we got lit up and wild at parties before the last couple of years had happened.

With every story, Clark talked less and less, and his head fell farther back on the chair, eventually coming to a stop as Michael was telling us about his friend Jordan from first grade. We listened to Clark's gravely snoring for just a minute before Camile leaned over and pushed him on the shoulder. He jerked his head up and stood, sluggish and mumbling something that sounded like "I'm goin', I'm goin'." Then he shuffled down the hallway and into his room. Michael did the same, telling me that he hoped I'd feel better in the morning. Camile shut the door, handed me the jug of water, and gave me a final dose of ibuprofen and the antibiotic. Then she climbed onto the other side of the bed and turned out the light.

"If you need anything, just yell," she said. I thanked her and said I would. In the dark now, I lay and wondered about what would happen in the coming months. I imagined never leaving the house to run again. I imagined having to stand strong on the front porch and brandish weapons to scare away attackers. I imagined moving to a new neighborhood that was just a little bit quieter and safer. I imagined seeing mom's face again and hearing her voice, low and whispery, singing, "I say a little prayer for yoouu." I wondered but didn't worry. Soon, Camile was asleep and breathing calmly beside me. Clark was just one room away. Michael was down the hall. And we rested, not alone in the dark and mild night.

About the Author

TYLER J. RIGG lives in Columbus, Ohio. He grew up in Northwest Ohio and attended Miami University. This is his first publication. You can read more of his work at:

https://litvaporware.wordpress.com.